His Life Abiding

Marsh Myers

Laughing Boy Fiction, 2013
Copyright © 2013 by Marsh Myers

This is a work of fiction. Any resemblance to actual persons,
living or dead, events, or locales is entirely coincidental.

ISBN: 0989071510
ISBN-13: 978-0-9890715-1-2

1. Teens - fiction
2. Teens - Science fiction & fantasy - fantasy

First edition
Printed in the United States of America
by Laughing Boy Fiction

For my sons,
Cooper and Myles,
with love.

CONTENTS

ACKNOWLEDGMENTS

I am deeply grateful to all the friends and colleagues
who have assisted and encouraged me over the years.

But in particular, much thanks and love to my
mother, father and sister – always my
loudest cheerleaders and greatest inspirations.

CHAPTER ONE

The plane's shadow had just passed along the surface of the U-boat when there was a great detonation several yards to the submarine's port side. A watery plume rose thirty feet into the air and threw cold spray across the boat's deck. The captain was yelling and gesturing wildly with both arms, but the concussion had left such a ringing in his ears Ehren could barely understand him. Off their starboard side, Ehren could see the crew members of the other U-boat scrambling along the deck, feverishly working to disconnect the refueling lines which coupled the two submarines. Refueling during daylight hours was always risky, but the other boat had been running on fumes and their captain had seen no alternative but to chance it. The periscopes had shown heavy banks of rain clouds which should have made it difficult for the American anti-submarine aircraft to see them. It had seemed a reasonable gamble and Ehren didn't take time to second-guess his captain's decision. Now, everything was focussed on disconnecting and reeling in the fuel lines so both U-boats could escape beneath the waves before more planes arrived.

Ehren climbed toward the back of the boat to help unhook the fueling line, but the turbulent seas and his own sense of panic made him clumsy and slow. Despite his ears still ringing from the explosion, he could detect the insect-like buzz of an approaching airplane. He looked up and saw three specks against the grey clouds as the planes circled around the U-boats like sharks around whales.

He reached the refueling line where several crew-mates were desperately trying to release the clamps and free the boats. The explosions had made the ocean even choppier and had forced the two vessels further apart, stretching the tethers between them almost to the breaking point. Ehren's vessel was already at a disadvantage. It was larger, heavier and slower than the other submarine, a supply ship rather than a sleek warship bristling with weapons. Even to the enemy pilots circling overhead, it must have seemed like the more desirable target. Ehren pulled on the fueling line with all his strength, hoping to provide enough slack so the clamps would release.

"What're they doing?" one of his comrades yelled, cuffing him on the shoulder.

Ehren glanced up. The men on the other boat had abandoned their posts and were scrambling along the deck and down the ladders into the submarine. They'd managed to release the fueling line from their side but the hose flailed in the water, disgorging a thick stream of petrol between the two ships. Now only one man remained on deck, a giant with a small head and thick limbs. He balanced himself carefully, raising a heavy ax above his head. He swung savagely. The blade clanged against the side of his vessel like a church bell as his first attempt missed widely.

"He's insane! He's trying to cut the lines!" Ehren shouted. Then to his comrades: "Get those valves shut! We're dumping fuel into the water!"

2

Another plane passed overhead, followed swiftly by the hollow plunk of a depth-charge and the pop and sizzle of bullets hitting the water nearby. The ocean convulsed in a great bubble as the explosive detonated and frigid water surged across both vessels. The two men next to Ehren vanished into the foam, swept from the U-boat's deck and swallowed up by the dark sea. Ehren felt his feet sweep out from under him and he flopped painfully on this stomach. He immediately rolled and caught the fuel line with both hands. Another wall of water rolled across the deck and for an instant Ehren felt weightless as the ocean lifted him from the U-boat's metal hull, then slammed him down again with a wet thud. His body was so cold he barely felt the pain of the impact. He glanced up at the conning tower, but his captain was no longer there. One side of the tower had been shredded by gunfire. On the other boat, the man with the ax also teetered to his feet as both submarines rocked and their hulls clanged together. A bright stream of blood had erupted from his left calve where a bullet had passed clean through. Despite the injury, he lifted the ax again.

"We can't submerge if the fuel valve is open! Help me release the clamps!" Ehren yelled across to the man.

The giant paused for an instant, glaring at Ehren from under heavy black brows. His expression betrayed what he would not take the time to shout back. There was no affinity there, no loyalty for his countrymen and fellow submariners, only the panicked look of a desperate animal. If he could do anything to help Ehren's boat, he'd chosen against it. Ehren knew immediately this was a race to see who secured his vessel first. Survival would be measured by the seconds he saved.

The ax began to clang against the metal hull again. The second strike severed one of the tethers which shot back toward Ehren like a bullwhip, missing him by *inches. Ehren dropped to the deck and kicked at the fuel line, trying to knock the clamps loose with the heel of his boot. The pungent odor of spilled diesel almost overwhelmed him. He held his breath kicked again. The clamp moved, but it was already too little too late. From the corner of his eye, he saw the man on the other sub toss away the ax as he half-limped, half-ran to an open hatch. The hatch slammed shut and almost immediately the other U-boat began to pull away.*

Ehren watched as the dark cylindrical shape slipped beneath the waves and in that instant his fear was replaced with despair. Strangely, his thoughts weren't for himself. They were for his parents back home in Germany. They'd never know what happened to him, he grieved. His name would just become another entry on a list of those whose burial at sea was without ceremony or witnesses. The drone of the war planes echoed in his ears. More depth charges erupted around him. Again the ocean lifted him, but this time there was nothing to grab and the water crushed him in its icy hand as his mouth filled with the taste of salt.

He had no idea of how long he was underwater. The liquid universe around him echoed with pings and pops. Then there was another detonation, closer this time, which bounced him back to the surface. He gasped and choked, throwing up brine only to inhale scalding steam. The current was pulling him away from the U-boat, but he could still see it well enough to know it was foundering, slowly rolling over on its starboard side as thick smoke belched from the conning tower. Some of his crew-mates had made it onto deck and were tossing themselves into the sea.

It wouldn't matter, Ehren thought. The frigid Atlantic will kill them almost as quickly as a sinking submarine.

Another blast — but this time Ehren was washed with a blinding heat rather than icy ocean spray. Bright orange flames skipped along the water's surface, as though the water had transformed into fire. He didn't try to swim. His waterlogged clothes, heavy boots and the unbelievable cold all conspired to pull his body under the waves. The heat subsided. The booms and pings and hisses faded. The normal sounds of the ocean returned and when Ehren looked again, there was no sign of the submarine except for some fading tendrils of smoke and steam.

He and a handful of crew-mates bobbed in the water, transfixed on the shimmering waves where their boat had been just a few seconds before. Then the insect-like hum returned. Against the clouds, Ehren could see the war-planes circling again.

He asked himself: Is this where I end? Will it be by bombs or bullets? Or will the planes just leave me and the others to die in the freezing Atlantic?

One of the planes turned toward them and came in low over the water's surface. It was dark blue with a large white star painted on the fuselage. Its wings were tipped with cannon muzzles and two unused bombs still hung from its belly. Ehren closed his eyes. The plane passed overhead. He felt its shadow on his face. There was a splash, but no detonation.

A dark bundle floated on the waves nearby. The other men were swimming toward it. A life boat.

Tyler was seated behind a row of boxwood shrubs waiting for the new kid to arrive. He liked to believe he and the family cat were the only members of the household who knew that if you squeezed down near the end of the porch and then wiggled in on your belly, there was a gap between the shrubs and the house spacious enough to accommodate an unusually tall 13-year-old boy, his flashlight and a box of crackers he'd stolen from the pantry. The cat, Phineas, had found the spot first. It was where he retreated on those rare occasions when someone forgot to close a window or a door and he was able to stretch his long, thin legs in the wilderness of the front yard. Tonight Phineas was safely contained inside, sitting on the window ledge above the hiding spot and mewing his displeasure at Tyler.

Although she allowed Tyler to believe his secret was intact, his foster mother Karen had known about the hiding place behind the boxwood shrubs for nearly a year. She figured it out the first time Tyler had disappeared. The cat had told her where he was just by sitting on the window ledge and making his deep, irritated meows. But Karen said nothing because she understood every boy wanted his own secret place, and for Tyler it was almost a necessity. Sometimes he hid there when the bad memories returned. Sometimes he hid there when he'd been in trouble at school again. Sometimes he hid there when a new child was being dropped off by a caseworker. Whatever the reason, Tyler only went behind the boxwoods when he was feeling overwhelmed.

Tyler was half finished with the crackers when a car bounced up the driveway. He squished down low and snapped off his flashlight. The caseworker got out first. She was a skinny lady with frizzy hair, dressed in a dark blue pantsuit and a colorful vest. She'd been to the house before, dropping off or picking up other children. And every time Tyler encountered her, she was wearing a vest. Sometimes the vests were very fancy, other times as plain as a bed sheet, but there was always a vest. Tyler couldn't remember her name but he'd never been very good at names anyway. Karen told him it was impolite for him to refer to everybody else in the world as "what's-his-name" or "that lady," so he began inventing new names for the people he couldn't remember. The first time this caseworker had come to the house, she had worn a vest covered with fringe and turquoise-colored beads and looked like she'd stepped out of a Hollywood Western. Ever since, Tyler remembered her as "The Cowgirl."

The Cowgirl went to the passenger's side of the car and opened it for the boy sitting inside. He was small with a thick dome of curly blond hair and large blue eyes. He was carrying a wooden train. The Cowgirl reached around him and pulled out the signature luggage of the foster child: large black garbage bags. Tyler remembered that he'd arrived at Karen's two years earlier with a similar bag slung over his shoulder. He didn't know which had made him sadder at the time: the fact that his entire world fit into a garbage bag or everything he owned was packaged like so much trash. He felt a moment of intense sympathy for the child standing there holding his train, but he quickly shook it off. He didn't like those kind of feelings. They made his heart ache.

The little boy gazed up at the house. "Why does it have a tower?" he asked.

The Cowgirl replied, "A hundred years ago, this used to be a working lighthouse. Inside that tower is a huge light ships could see far out in the ocean. When they saw the light, they knew there were rocks ahead and they should steer clear."

She took him by the hand and led him up to the porch. Karen had already opened the front door and greeted them in her best singsong voice. The child looked uncomfortable and for a moment glanced over at the boxwoods where Tyler was hidden. The look on his face was a combination of amusement and curiosity. Can he see me, Tyler wondered? It seemed like their eyes met, if only for an instant. Tyler hunched even lower and reassured himself that he was completely invisible. After all, only the cat knew about the secret spot.

The screen door on the porch banged shut and the voices receded inside. After a moment or two, Karen reappeared and yelled, "Tyler, time to come in!" She never looked over at the boxwoods.

Tyler knew he had a reputation for being difficult. His therapist called it "oppositional defiant disorder." He didn't understand what that meant exactly, but it seem to be the grownup way of saying he didn't like following instructions, especially if the instructions were coming from an adult. Tyler would argue that all eighth grade boys had a touch of oppositional defiant disorder, and that he was just particularly good at it. Sometimes his defiance would be small, like refusing to eat his Brussels sprouts at dinner time. Other times it was large, like when he crawled under the auditorium stage at school and refused to come out for forty-five minutes. The assistant principal and the janitor finally had to crawl in after him and pull him out by his ankles. Now that Karen had called him inside, Tyler automatically went into defiant-mode. As a matter of routine, he was careful to never respond too quickly to Karen's requests, but he had the added pleasure of making The Cowgirl and the new child wait on him too. Even Phineas, who was probably the second-most defiant member of the household just because he was a cat, had run off to meet the new arrival. But Tyler decided to wait, slowly licking the salt off of each remaining cracker, then sneaking around to the back of the house and walking in with his best "Oh-I-forgot-you-were-coming" look on his face.

The child was seated on the floor petting Phineas, ignoring the adult conservation around him. His garbage bags and toy train were thrown into a heap near the front door. He was introduced as Sawyer, but Tyler immediately forgot the name and would spend the rest of the night referring to the 8-year-old as "the new kid" or "that kid" or sometimes just as "him."

"Isn't this a nice house, Sawyer?" The Cowgirl asked, trying to draw the child's attention away from the purring feline.

Sawyer didn't answer. The cat was much more interesting than the old, creaky building.

"Tyler, why don't you take Sawyer upstairs and show him his new bedroom?" Karen suggested.

"Don't wanna," Tyler replied. Those words had come out of his mouth so smoothly he hadn't even realized it. Actually, he did want to take "the new kid" upstairs. It was the perfect time to check out what he had in those big garbage bags. But now he was stuck. One of Tyler's rules for being difficult was never agree to something once you have refused to do it... even if you really wanted to.

"I'll do it, Mom," Griffin said.

Griffin was Karen's son, her only child from a bad marriage which ended years ago. He was eighteen ("practically nineteen" as he was quick to remind everyone) and was constructed like a Manga comic book character with a plume of spiked black hair and large, bright green eyes. He was short for his age, and his arms and legs seemed unusually long. He moved with a strange fluidity which reminded Tyler of a monkey swinging between limbs on a tree.

Just like with wild animals, there was always a pecking order among the children in the lighthouse based on age and longevity. Griffin was the first and oldest child, and therefore lived comfortably at the top of the pecking order, dispensing his wisdom and receiving the admiring looks of all the younger boys who passed through Karen's house. Accordingly, he lived in the loftiest place available: a split-level bedroom which had originally been the lighthouse's top two floors. Tyler placed himself second in the pecking order. He'd come to Karen's house two years earlier and was still there. He couldn't remember how many other kids had called the lighthouse their temporary home in that time. Maybe twenty? Some had moved onto other foster homes. Some were adopted. A few lucky ones returned home to their real parents, whom the caseworkers referred to as "bio mom" or "bio dad." But month after month, Tyler stayed put. It used to bother him that so many other kids had come and gone and he was still there. He finally decided it was due to his reputation for being difficult. Foster and adoptive parents didn't want difficult children any more than "bio parents" did. He finally decided it would be okay if he spent the rest of his childhood at Karen's lighthouse. After all, it put him higher in the pecking order and he was able to get a bigger bedroom.

Now that Griffin had trumped Tyler by volunteering to take "the new kid" for a tour, Tyler felt obligated to mope around behind them, looking uninterested as he tried to overhear every word they said.

The lower floors of the lighthouse smelled of wood and old paint, the faintly bitter aroma of great age and generations of use. The rooms were small and, by modern standards, impractical. Karen told Tyler how, when she first bought the historic structure, she had to get rid of half of her furniture because it was too big to fit through the narrow doorways. But the building's design, with its small interconnected chambers and low ceilings, had been very practical for its nineteenth century residents. After all, if you lived on the tip of a rocky headland, battered constantly by wind and rainstorms, keeping warm would've been one of your first concerns. At that time, the entire building was heated by fireplaces and coal-burning stoves. A modern furnace system hadn't be added until the 1960s, but still the lighthouse could be drafty and cold when the Atlantic turned stormy. Over time, Tyler had come to love the building's unique qualities, even if it meant being a little chilly from time to time. He loved how the smooth floorboards creaked under his feet, making sure he could never sneak down to the bathroom in the middle of the night without everyone hearing him. He loved sitting in front of the fireplace on rainy nights when Phineas would curl up in his lap. He loved opening all his bedroom windows on a muggy summer's day and letting the ocean breeze waft across him. And sometimes, when he was all alone, he'd just stand in the hallway and listen to the building, as though he might hear the voices of its former residents.

But for the new kid, the lighthouse was just weird.

Sawyer followed Griffin up to the second floor and down the hall to an immense room cleverly arranged with bunk beds, couches and desks. Originally two separate rooms, Karen had removed a wall and created a huge space suitable for housing up to four boys. There was a connecting bathroom, three closets and a carpeted space lined with overstuffed pillows and plastic crates filled with toys. Karen called this area "the rumpus room." When Tyler had first arrived, this had been the room where he'd slept. It had taken him months to work up the nerve to ask Karen where the "rumpus" was and if he could play with it. She had to explain it was just a silly name for a play area for children. Tyler was annoyed the new kid understood what a "rumpus room" was immediately.

Sawyer kicked off his shoes and rubbed his dirty socks against the hardwood floor.

"Can we slide on this?" he asked Griffin.

The older boy shrugged and replied, "Just as long as mom doesn't catch you or you don't bash in your head on the furniture."

"I won't. I'm very good at sliding. Watch me."

Sawyer started to run across the floor and then slid about two feet. He skidded in a straight line over to the bedroom windows which looked east, down onto the cove and across the ocean. Along the horizon, dark twists of clouds were beginning to form.

He looked at Griffin and said, "A storm."

"Yup."

"I don't like storms, do you?"

Griffin shrugged. "They don't bother me. You have to get used to them when you live right next to the ocean."

Sawyer slid around several times in a big circle, making sure he had Griffin's full attention each time. Griffin was laughing, which also irritated Tyler. So the new kid could slide around in a circle, he fumed. What's so hilarious?

"Do you pee the bed?" Tyler asked the boy suddenly.

"Dude," Griffin frowned, "shut up."

"I don't pee the bed," Sawyer replied, continuing his sliding exercises without interruption.

Tyler went to the bunk beds and climbed onto the top mattress. "If you pee the bed you're not allowed to lie about it," he said sternly. "You don't get in trouble unless you try to hide it or lie about it. And you have to help clean it up, that's the rule."

"I don't pee the bed," Sawyer repeated.

"All foster kids pee the bed."

"Not me."

"Were you in the group home before here?"

"Yeah."

"Then you totally pee the bed. Everyone pees the bed in group homes. I peed the bed when I was in the group home."

"You've peed the bed here, too," Griffin added.

"Not anymore. I got over it."

"Well, good," Griffin said. "And if Sawyer pees the bed, I'm sure he'll get over it too. Either way, it's none of your biz."

"Yes it is. I sleep next door. I don't want to smell his pee all night."

"Tyler, there have been other kids in this house who've peed the bed. We'll deal with it. You don't have to be such a jerk."

"I don't pee the bed," Sawyer repeated, just in case no one had heard him the first two times.

"Don't worry about it," Griffin said. "Do you wanna see my room?"

Sawyer eagerly followed Griffin up the narrow staircase at the back of the house. It had lots of twists and turns and their footsteps echoed hollowly throughout the house. The boy already understood what an honor it was to be invited up to the teenager's room. Tyler lingered behind them, pausing on the landing which overlooked the living room to eavesdrop on Karen and The Cowgirl. As he expected, they were whispering about Sawyer. There was the usual stuff the adults always spoke about. There was the exchange of medications and paperwork and signatures. Then The Cowgirl began to speak about Sawyer's past and Tyler crouched down in the shadows to listen.

"I know you spoke to the therapist about his phobias," The Cowgirl said, "so I hope you're feeling comfortable with all this."

Tyler frowned. Phobias, huh? Foster children could have all kinds of strange fears. Once, a boy named Keith had lived with them for two weeks. He had a phobia about loud banging noises. Tyler had tried to drive him crazy by bouncing a tennis ball in the hallway outside him room in the middle of the night. Keith left the following day. Tyler was grounded for a month but he still thought it was pretty funny.

"I think we'll be fine," Karen answered. "I read over his entire packet, so I have a pretty clear understanding of his challenges."

Tyler chuckled. After years of living in the foster care system, he had learned the adults had a special language when it came to discussing children. For example, foster kids didn't have problems, they had "challenges." Sometimes, if things got really bad, they had "issues." If their problems got better, then they had "challenges" again. Griffin told him that all the foster parents, caseworkers and therapists attended classes where they learned to speak like this because it's not polite to say a child is nuts. Tyler didn't agree with Griffin. Over the years, he'd felt many things, but he never felt crazy. He just felt like he had, well, issues. But he excused Griffin's opinion. After all, the older boy had never been abandoned by a parent, never lived in a group home or bounced from placement to placement because his behavior was so awful no one could stand living with him for longer than a few months at a time. Griffin couldn't really understand the concept of "issues," even though he tried.

"So we don't really know what sets him off, right?" Karen asked.

"In my experience, it's been pretty random," The Cowgirl said. "Or maybe no one's just figured out the trigger yet. When he goes off you'll know it, believe me. Hopefully, in time, he'll be able to talk to you about it. But so far, he just loses control and it's hard for him to settle back down. Have you talked to your boys about this yet?"

"No, not yet. I didn't want them to have some bias toward Sawyer before they met him. You remember what Tyler did to that boy Keith?"

"Oh, yes. The ball bouncing incident."

"Yeah. We don't need anything like that again. I need to approach it very carefully. I'll probably discuss it with them tomorrow."

"Good." The Cowgirl looked at her watch. "I better go. Give me a call if there's anything you need. You have the emergency number, right?"

"Yeah, I'm all set. Thanks for all your help," Karen said, walking her to the front door.

"Tell Sawyer I said goodbye. I don't know where he went off to."

"They must be in the tower. I just heard them banging up the stairs. Drive carefully. It looks like there's a storm coming."

As Tyler snuck off to join the others in Griffin's room, he felt proud of this newfound knowledge. The new kid must be the mother of all bed-wetters, he told himself. He made a mental note to check Sawyer's sheets in the morning. He'd enjoy ratting him out to Karen.

Griffin's bedroom was tall, narrow and had a twisted iron staircase which led from one floor to the next. The ceiling and walls were covered in hundred-year-old wood paneling that had been painted and repainted so many times it had a smooth, rubbery look. The area seemed much larger during the day thanks to the abundance of windows. Windows everywhere, on every wall facing in every direction. The people who used to operate the lighthouse needed all the windows so they had a clear a view of the entire coastline. Directly above Griffin's room was the platform where the old spinning light still sat. Karen kept that part of the tower locked, but Griffin and Tyler had discovered the padlock was defective. If you yanked down on it hard enough, it would snap right open. Sometimes the two of them would sneak up there at night and it felt like you were floating among the stars.

When Griffin had first approached Karen about moving into the tower permanently, she agreed only if he first sound-proofed the area. Eighteen-year-olds made too much noise to be overhead from everyone else, she told him. So Griffin and his friends came up with a plan to carpet and insulate the tower. When they were done, the area was more livable, less drafty, and considerably quieter. To brighten the space during the nighttime hours, Griffin strung rows of large decorative lights along the rafters. Because he was short for his age, these hanging light bulbs presented no problem. But every time someone of height entered the tower — someone like Tyler — they were constantly bumping their heads against the lights, which would cause the whole room to flicker.

Griffin's bed didn't fit in the space, so he'd improvised by slinging a hammock from rafter to rafter.

Sleeping that way had taken some getting use to. When the storms blew in, the tower would sway and the hammock would rock. Griffin described it like sleeping on-board a ship at sea. Sawyer climbed up in it and was swinging happily.

"Your room smells funny," he said to no one in particular.

"You're smelling the light," Griffin replied, gesturing toward the ceiling. "When they still used this place as a lighthouse, they used oil in the light. Sometimes you can still smell it."

"It smells like a boat," Sawyer said, wrinkling his nose as he rocked in the hammock.

"How does it smell like a boat?"

"You know, like a submarine? Submarines smell like this inside 'cause of all the engines and stuff."

"That's not true," Tyler said. "I've been on a submarine and it didn't smell."

Sawyer laughed and said, "When were you on a submarine?"

"Uh, there happens to be one at a museum we went to on vacation. It was when we went to California. Right, Griff?"

Griffin nodded. "That's true. But I don't remember what it smelled like."

"Well some submarines smelled like oil," Sawyer said. "Old ones."

"How old was the submarine we went on, Griff?" Tyler asked.

"I don't know. It was a Russian submarine. It must have been about thirty or forty years old, I guess."

"Well, I'm talking about older subs," Sawyer said. "The insides would get filled up with smells and exhaust and then they'd have to go up to the surface of the water and open all the hatches to let fresh air in. Or sometimes they'd have these things called snorkels on them which they could raise up out of the water and that would let fresh air in, too."

"Snorkels? That's stupid. Submarines weren't invented before forty years ago and they didn't have snorkels on them," Tyler said. He didn't know any of this for certain and was trusting the new kid didn't either.

"Yes, they did," Sawyer insisted. "They've been around for a long, long time. Some had snorkels so the crews could get fresh air without having to surface."

Griffin chuckled. "You're like a walking encyclopedia, Sawyer," he said.

Sawyer shrugged. "I know a lot about submarines."

"Whatever," Tyler answered. "Your caseworker left."

Sawyer was about to respond, but a clap of thunder and the sound of rain hitting the tower windows distracted him.

"Storm's here," he said, jumping off the hammock. "Let's go downstairs."

"Why?" Tyler asked. "It's just thunder."

Sawyer walked quickly to the attic door. "I told you," he said, "I don't like storms."

CHAPTER TWO

In the days that followed Sawyer's arrival, Tyler had managed to compile a huge amount of information regarding the boy. For example, he knew Sawyer preferred to go to bed early and get up early so he could watch television before leaving for school. He could polish off an entire box of Cinnamon Toast Crunch singlehandedly. He talked way too much for a normal person and asked too many questions. When he wasn't asking questions, he was telling you a bunch of stuff about things that no one cared about anyway. He didn't like rainstorms or the ocean, but he did like singing, drawing and playing with Legos. He also responded favorably to Tyler's favorite game, "Guess which Matchbox car is in my mouth?"

Two days after his arrival, Tyler had offered to help Sawyer unpack his garbage bags. The child had very few toys and most of them were mismatched, damaged or just downright strange (like a plastic frog that played "It's A Grand Ol' Flag" and the left arm off a Barbie doll). The wooden train was Sawyer's most cherished item. He told Tyler it had been the last Christmas gift his "bio mom" had ever given him. Tyler understood the preciousness of such a gift and placed it on a high shelf where it would be safe.

The remainder of the bags contained clothes and lots of them. This was another obvious sign that Sawyer had been in group homes. Tyler remembered from his early days in foster care that clothes (like mismatched toys) were always donated to group homes in large quantities, mainly by families whose kids enjoyed both loving parents and the luxury of buying things new. These hand-me-downs were given out to the foster children based more on size than on need. As a result, Tyler once ended up with sixteen pairs of pants but no shirts. Sawyer had an unusual number of jackets, and some of them, Tyler was certain, had originally belonged to girls. Sawyer spent ten minutes trying to cram all his clothes into one drawer, until Tyler pointed out that he had a whole set of drawers and a closet he could use. This too was the sign of a kid from group homes — where space was carefully rationed and children were housed as many as six to a room.

One other fact about Sawyer had become very apparent during the first few days: he didn't like to bathe. He had been able to trick Karen for the first couple of nights by wetting down his hair in the sink and putting on his terry cloth robe before leaving the bathroom. Tyler had to compliment him on the effort. He was smart enough to stay in the bathroom with the shower running for at least ten minutes. Other kids had blown the lie by leaving the bathroom too soon, but Sawyer was smarter than most. On the third day, he tried to disguise his own stink by rubbing himself down with vanilla-scented hand lotion. It was a good effort and something Tyler had never thought of, but it still didn't work.

"Dude," Griffin had teased him, "what good is putting on lotion if you still stink? That's like spraying perfume on a dog turd. It's still a dog turd and everybody knows it. You don't want to be a dog turd, do you?"

By the fourth and fifth day, Sawyer's smell had become particularly bad. Tyler had noticed his greasy hair was leaving marks on the sofa and pillows, so Karen decided to deal with the situation in her usual manner. Without a raised voice, she informed Sawyer that as long as he didn't bathe he would not be allowed to participate in certain activities. Outings and play-time with other kids was out of the question, naturally, and at meal time he had to sit at a little folding table in the hallway so his stink wouldn't ruin any appetites. For a kid who loved being the center of attention as much as Sawyer, these punishments seemed particularly cruel. All Karen had to do was sit back and wait for him to crack.

By the sixth day, Sawyer had stolen a can of spray deodorant from Griffin's room and had doused his clothes in it. No one bought it and he lost his television privileges for a week for being a thief. Then, despite his fear of storms, he deliberately stayed out in the rain and claimed it counted as a shower. No one bought that either. In between, he pouted, threw tantrums, and called Karen a variety of curse words Tyler had never heard before nor understood. But Karen had been a foster mother for a very long time. She was immune to all of it. She didn't budge an inch.

With Sawyer being only a day or two away from actually attracting flies, Tyler decided it was his personal duty to make sure the boy bathed before nightfall.

Obviously, negotiation was futile so Tyler turned to deceit. In preparation for this, he rummaged through the house until he came up with a handful of bath beads, some small soaps shaped like sea shells and half a bottle of strawberry-scented bubble bath. He tossed these into the bottom of the tub in the upstairs bathroom and started the water running. Almost immediately a heavy foam began to rise and the swirling clouds of soap began to darken the water to a deep violet. Then came the super-soaker squirt guns. The larger of the two could hold almost two liters of liquid. Tyler knew this for a fact because Griffin had once filled it with Dr. Pepper and spent the next hour shooting it into his mouth. The super-soakers were the key. They were toys no eight-year-old could resist.

With the tub filled and the super-soakers at the ready, Tyler marched down the hall to find Sawyer. The child was sitting in the "rumpus room" surrounded by piles of colorful Legos. No flies yet, Tyler noted.

"What're you building?" Tyler asked.

Sawyer held up his creation. It was a long vehicle with numerous fins. "Submarine," he said proudly.

"Submarine. Right. You're crazy for submarines," he said. Then he put his hands on his hips and said in his sternest voice, "Okay, I'm gonna tell you something but you have to keep a secret."

Sawyer was immediately intrigued and put aside his plastic creation. "What?"

"I'll show you my secret weapons if you want to play with me?"

Sawyer smiled. "Secret weapons? Like what a cop or an army man would have?"

"No. Like what a secret spy would have. You can even make up a spy name for yourself if you want. Who do you want to be?"

"I don't know. Sawyer?"

"You have to come up with a different name, stupid. You can't use your real name."

"But I like my name."

"Spies don't use their real names. If they did, their enemies would just be able to look them up on the internet and blow up their house."

"I like my name," Sawyer insisted.

Tyler sighed. Clearly, Sawyer was going to be a long-term project. "Okay, okay. You're Sawyer the Spy. Come on."

The two boys crept down the hallway to the bathroom and Tyler closed the door behind them. The super-soakers lay on the floor in their neon-plastic glory. Sawyer made a low gulping sound at the sight of them.

"I've made a secret potion that'll turn us invisible," Tyler said, leading him over to the bathtub. The foam hissed softly and the steam rising off of the water smelled like warm strawberries. It was almost enough to mask the stench rising off of Sawyer, Tyler thought. Almost.

"Don't witches make potions?" Sawyer asked. "I thought we were spies?"

"I said secret potion, moron," Tyler snapped. "Secret agents make secret potions. Witches make regular potions. Got it?"

"Yeah."

"Fill your gun."

Sawyer did as he was told. Then Tyler stood back and ordered, "Now spray me!"

Without thinking twice, Sawyer immediately began to douse the older boy. Once the front of his shirt and pants were completely wet, Tyler turned around and allowed Sawyer to saturate the rest of him. The eight-year-old was laughing hysterically, apparently unconcerned about the growing puddle on the bathroom floor.

"Okay, now it's your turn," Tyler said. To his surprise, his plan was working perfectly. Sawyer stood there and allowed himself to be soaked head to foot, giggling the entire time.

Tyler frowned and said, "Something's wrong. I can still see you. Can you see me?"

Sawyer nodded.

"Clearly we've not used enough of the secret potion." And with that, Tyler dunked the gun again, refilled it, and emptied onto Sawyer. By this time, a river of sudsy water was snaking down the hallway toward the stairs. It was Phineas the cat who noticed it first, curling himself around the banister and watching with fascination as the water dribbled from one step onto another.

Griffin, who'd been watching television downstairs, wondered why the house suddenly smelled of warm strawberries and then noticed the growing pool of lavender-colored water at the base of the stairs. He ran upstairs and for a moment just stood at the bathroom door, his mouth open, frozen with disbelief.

"What have you done!" he yelled at Tyler as he snatched the super-soakers out of their hands.

"I didn't do nothing!" Tyler yelled back. Didn't Griffin know he wasn't supposed to yell, Tyler fumed? Yelling just got his hackles up faster and then you were in a fight you couldn't possibly win. By the time Karen arrived, Tyler was in full attack-mode.

"Are you completely retarded? Look at the mess you made!" Griffin yelled, grabbing Tyler by the arm.

"Let go of me, butt-crack!" Tyler screamed back, yanking himself out of Griffin's grip. "I didn't do nothing! We were just playing spies!"

"Spies? What are you talking about, you idiot?"

Karen laid a hand quietly on Griffin's shoulder. She quickly spotted the empty bottle of bubble bath and the half-dissolved soaps lying in the bottom of the tub and understood Tyler's intent. His execution of the idea was sloppy as usual, but part of her admired his ingenuity.

"All right, boys," she said, "I think it goes without saying that squirt guns are only used outside. Now, you've both made this mess so you both need to clean it up before it ruins the floors. Go get the mop and some paper towels. Afterward, both of you shower all the soap off and change out of your wet clothes."

In the days that followed, Tyler found the punishment they shared seemed to make Sawyer like him more. The younger boy never blamed him for the loss of his television or video game privileges. Nor did he resent having to take double-duty on cleaning Phineas's cat box. All the bother seemed worth it, because suddenly Sawyer had what every little kid really wanted — the undivided attention of an older boy.

With little else to occupy their time, Tyler escorted the boy all around the property and even took him down the narrow winding path to the rocky beach below the lighthouse. Sawyer was reluctant to approach the shore, apparently bothered by the crashing waves and the cold spray which swept over them.

"Do you want to look for crabs under the rocks?" Tyler suggested.

Sawyer shook his head and shuddered. "I don't like the noise," he stammered.

Tyler shrugged and led him back up the hillside. They spent the next hour exploring some of the old structures which surrounded the lighthouse but had now slipped into decay. The lighthouse's architecture was unusual since the light keeper's house and the tower were part of the same structure, a five-story construction with white clapboard sides, decorative scroll work along the eaves and tall red brick chimneys at either end. But there were two other structures on the property as well, both dating to the late-nineteenth century and now quite hazardous. Naturally, Tyler visited these buildings often.

The first of these ruins was a wooden shack which once housed the light keeper's tools and oil reserves. The shed leaned dangerously to one side and part of the roof had collapsed. The tiny building was empty, but Tyler still liked to crawl around inside as he would occasionally find a rusted nail, auger bit or saw blade lying hidden among the warped floorboards now being split apart by tufts of yellow grass. He'd once found an old brass funnel just outside the shack's door. Karen told him it was surely over a century old and probably used by the last light keeper to live on the property. The funnel now sat on Tyler's bookcase as a prized possession.

Behind the shack was Tyler's favorite off-limits ruin: a large metal cistern which had supplied water to the lighthouse residents and building's steam-powered foghorn. Once modern plumbing had been installed in the early twentieth century, the cistern became unnecessary but no one had bothered to remove it. There was not much to look at, as most of the reservoir was underground and only a circular cover with a small hatch was visible. But Tyler liked how the steel had become discolored and the rivets along its upper edge dripped with rust.

"Listen to this," Tyler said, jumping up and down on the cistern's lid. The metal rumbled beneath his feet like a giant drum. "Do you hear it?"

Sawyer shook his head. "What?" he asked.

"Listen," Tyler sighed. He crouched down and with great effort managed to open the ancient hatch and let it bang against the metal cover like a hammer striking an anvil. A cold breath smelling of mildew washed over his face. Below it was inky black, as though he was looking straight through the Earth and into space. Tyler jumped again and the cistern rang more loudly this time as its rusted skin shuddered. The sound frightened Sawyer and he took several steps backward.

"Do you hear the water in there?" Tyler asked. "Hear it sloshing around? It's been in there for, like, a hundred years."

"I don't like that open," Sawyer told him.

"Why?"

"I don't know. Close it."

"Geeze, you're such a 'fraidy!"

Tyler picked up a large rock lying nearby and squatted over the open hole. He lifted the stone above the opening but then paused. The cistern exhaled again. The smell of deep, chilled water and corroding metal made him shiver, but he didn't know why. He'd been to the cistern dozens of times before and never felt that sensation before. Sawyer was clearly creeping him out.

He dropped the rock. It seemed to take forever to hit the water inside. It made a loud plunking noise.

"That rock will never see daylight again," Tyler said to no one in particular. "Not in a million years."

"Tyler, I wanna leave," Sawyer protested, but Tyler dismissed him.

"There's nothing to be scared of. It's just old, that's all."

"You might fall in and get trapped. Trapped forever. Just like the rock!"

"I don't think I could fit down there. The opening's too small. But look, it's okay," he said. And with that, he crouched down and shoved his right arm up to the shoulder into the opening. He wiggled his fingers. It was cold inside, like a freezer.

"Stop!" Sawyer yelled.

Tyler felt his delinquent qualities bubbling forth, the side of him which liked to make other people squirm. Sawyer was suddenly like a worm on a hook and he couldn't help himself. "Wanna see me put my head inside there?" he grinned roguishly.

"No! Please stop! I wanna go back to the house."

"Why? Do you think something will bite it off?"

"Tyler!"

Tyler dropped to all fours and positioned his head over the hatch. The weathered metal groaned under his weight. He couldn't see a thing inside and for an instant there was some glimmer of common sense which made him pause. But he dismissed common sense just as was ignored Sawyer's cries.

He shut his eyes and lowered his head. He had to move it slightly from side to side to make it fit through the hatch. The cold, clammy air choked him. He stayed like that for several seconds until he summoned up the courage to open his eyes. Blackness. He had a morbid thought about what it would be like to be trapped in there, inside a giant metal shell filled with water, cut off from sunshine and warmth forever and ever.

Suddenly the entire cistern trembled, as though all the water inside shifted like a great wave. Tyler lost his balance and pitched forward, his neck scraping painfully along the edge of the hatch. Then something caught him around the shirt collar and he felt himself being tossed off the metal platform and into the weeds nearby. When he looked up, Griffin was standing over him.

"Are you capable of even going a day without getting into trouble?" the older boy growled. "You know you're not supposed to be playing around this thing!"

"And you know you're not supposed to be going up to the light," Tyler responded defiantly, pointing at the tower. "If you're so worried about everyone following the rules, how come you're always messing around with that broken lock?"

"The light isn't dangerous, Tyler. Mom doesn't like the height so that's why she keeps it shut up, but it's not falling apart like these damn old ruins."

"I told him he might fall in," Sawyer called from a distance. He had run halfway back to the house.

"Looks like he almost did," Griffin sneered. "Then what would you have done?"

Tyler curled his lip and replied sarcastically, "I would have drowned."

"Go back to the house with Sawyer," Griffin ordered. "I'll be there in a moment."

The two younger boys trudged to the lighthouse's front porch and watched as Griffin dragged a length of heavy chain and a padlock out of the basement and sealed the cistern's lid for good.

Although irritated, Tyler didn't worry about the cistern being chained shut or sitting through the boring lecture on safety he got from Karen later that evening. Instead, his mind kept replaying Sawyer's panicked reaction. And Tyler found himself wondering more and more why the boy was so scared of such strange things.

CHAPTER THREE

Two U.S. naval officers entered the room. They wore khaki uniforms and set their caps and two stacks of file folders on the table top. They didn't say anything. They didn't even bother to make eye contact or acknowledge Ehren was in the room and had been sitting there, alone, for over an hour. They slid their chairs noisily across the tile floor and opened their folders. Ehren saw a short stack of photographs paper-clipped to the inside of the covers. One was his official prisoner of war mug shot, taken just a few hours after he'd been rescued from the cold waters of the Atlantic. He still had his beard in the photo, but the Americans had made him shave it off soon after. The other photos were of he and his comrades as they had been off-loaded from the warship which had rescued them. A naval officer wearing a tan uniform and a wide-brimmed helmet had met the survivors at the bottom of the gangplank and had snapped numerous photos as they ambled off the ship, filed into buses and were driven to the massive military complex Ehren now called home. At the time, he assumed the photos were for propaganda purposes and would be published in a local newspaper under a headline about a brave American victory at sea.

Apparently, however, the Americans had something else in mind.

"Good morning," one of the naval officers said to him in German. "I am Lieutenant Spolarich and this is Major Sharpe. I understand you speak English, Prisoner-of-War Tschantz?"

"Yes," Ehren replied in English. "My mother and father spoke English. We spoke it at home along with German."

The naval officer smiled slightly and asked, "Good. That'll make things easier. Are you comfortable continuing this conversation in English?"

"Yes."

"Excellent. Can you read and write English as well?" Lieutenant Spolarich asked while scratching notes with a dull pencil in the margins of his paperwork.

"Yes, but not as well as I speak," Ehren said.

"Are you a Nazi, Prisoner-of-War Tschantz?"

"I don't understand..."

The Lieutenant looked annoyed. Ehren expected his captors to treat him poorly. After all, his country had been at war with the United States for almost three years and the U-boats were infamous among the Americans. Every ship sailing the Atlantic Ocean feared them. But he was also frightened by the questions he was being asked. Are these officers trying to trap me, he asked himself? If I answer wrong, will I be locked up in a cell somewhere for the rest of the war? Or put against a wall and shot?

Lieutenant Spolarich repeated the question with deliberate and sarcastic care: "Are... you... a... member of the National... Socialist... German Worker's Party... Prisoner-of-War Tschantz? Are you a member of the Nazi party?"

"No," Ehren said quickly. "Not a member of the party. My father went to the prison camps."

The officer raised an eyebrow. "Your father was imprisoned by the Nazis? Why?"

A lump had formed in Ehren's throat. It was still painful to talk about it. "He voted wrong. He spoke out. He didn't like what Nazis were doing to people of Germany. So one night the police came and banged on our door and said 'You will come with us!' My father went away for two years. Later we found out it was our neighbor who turned him in, who told the police that he was a traitor to the Fuhrer. When my father came home, he was very sad. Broken. Now he can barely walk and he's always ill. They took his soul away."

Lieutenant Spolarich scribbled more notes and underlined several words. Then he asked, "But you still wore their uniform, Prisoner-of-War Tschantz. You served aboard one of their U-boats and waged war for Hitler. Doesn't that make you a Nazi?"

"No," Ehren said firmly. "Not a Nazi. At home, you serve in the military or you go to the camps. Sometimes you are killed. I was drafted at seventeen and sent to the submarine school. Aboard my boat, there were others. Two of my comrades weren't even German, they were Polish. They were forced to serve in our navy because there is a shortage of men now."

"But when you were drafted, you still went to the submariners' school, didn't you? You could've refused. You could've run away."

"There is no place to run that secret police cannot find you. My father said to me, 'Ehren, if you serve in the military at least you have the chance to live, to survive the war. If you refuse, they will take you to the camps and you will never be seen again.' So I went and I served."

More notes were written. The two officers whispered to each other and then wrote some more.

Major Sharpe closed his folder and looked straight into Ehren's eyes. "Thank you for your time, Prisoner-of-War Tschantz," he said. "We will be speaking with you again."

The day after the incident at the cistern, Sawyer's caseworker had returned to the lighthouse carrying a large bundle of folders. She was wearing a vest which looked like a bedroom quilt covered in large sunflowers. Her arrival made Tyler apprehensive. He knew from bitter experience that there were only two times caseworkers showed up unexpectedly at the house: when something had gone very wrong and when a child was being removed. Tyler wasn't sure which occasion this was and in an instant he was terrified that his days at the lighthouse might be over. It didn't seem fair if The Cowgirl was here to remove him. After all, he'd done reasonably well in Karen's care. There hadn't been any visits to the emergency room in over a year and he no longer found it necessary to smash lamps in order to make his point during an argument.

See, he thought, that's progress.

Although he was told to stay in his room, Tyler snuck out and perched at the top of the stairway so he could overhear the conversation between The Cowgirl, Karen and Griffin. He could see the back of The Cowgirl's head and her left shoulder. She was writing as she talked, filling out official-looking carbonless forms and then separating them into stacks of yellow, pink and white sheets.

Karen was speaking: "I don't believe for a moment that Tyler was trying to endanger Sawyer. But you know how he likes to mess with their heads, too. It's like a game for him."

"I don't believe he was trying to endanger Sawyer either," replied The Cowgirl. "But I'm concerned that he might accidentally hurt Sawyer if this is how he's chosen to play around him. Tyler has a long history of being very rough with other kids. We don't want a repeat of the YMCA incident, right?"

Tyler's mouth fell open. The YMCA incident, he thought? Was she really bringing that up? It had been two years and everyone in the world had forgotten about the YMCA incident except The Cowgirl. You push one kid down some stairs and you're labeled for life!

A small fire began to burn in Tyler's chest. He wondered why the adults always had to focus on the bad stuff?

"Sawyer wasn't actually anywhere near the cistern," Griffin said. "He was afraid of it. When Tyler lost his balance, the kid took off running. As for the thing in the bathroom with the super-soakers, I think he was just trying to get Sawyer to bathe. It's like that kid's allergic to water and soap."

"That's true. Tyler was pretty upset about that," Karen said. "The other night he was demanding that I make Sawyer bathe somehow, which is hilarious because you remember how little Tyler bathed when he first came here?"

The three of them shared a brief laugh at Tyler's expense. It was at that moment Tyler felt certain there was conspiracy in the air. His suspicions seemed to be confirmed the following afternoon when Karen packed him up and drove him into town for an "emergency meeting" with Dr. Cardenas.

Dr. Cardenas was a psychiatrist who worked with Child Protective Services. Nearly every boy or girl in CPS care had visits with him at some time or another... and Tyler hadn't found one yet who liked him. The doctor was built like a stick-figure with a large, egg-shaped head, a patchy beard and giant gold-rimmed glasses. There were several things about Dr. Cardenas that Tyler had figured out from day one:

First, Dr. Cardenas would forget Tyler's name even though he had his chart sitting in his lap. Most of the time he called him "Kevin." For several months the previous year he had called him "Michael." And once and only once he'd inexplicably called him "Priscilla."

Second, Dr. Cardenas had an office full of toys and children's books which no child had ever been allowed to touch. Tyler knew this because of the thick layer of dust on every game board, puzzle, action figure and miniature car in the place. Several years earlier, he'd become obsessed with playing with a fire engine with a retractable ladder. For months he tried every trick he knew to get ahold of the toy. Finally, he asked Dr. Cardenas how and when he could play with the truck.

"After you've sat and spoken with me, and if you're a good boy, then I will let you play with the fire truck," the man replied.

Tyler spent the next forty-five minutes in the greatest display of patience and cooperation ever seen in that office, but when his session was over Dr. Cardenas still hurried him out of the room before the fire truck could be pulled from its dusty shelf. After that, Tyler realized the toys in Dr. Cardenas's office were a decoy designed to make caseworkers and foster parents believe he was a "kid person" when in reality he didn't seem to like them much.

This time, however, Dr. Cardenas was particularly grim-faced with Tyler. He sat in his leather chair with Tyler's file lying open in his lap, chewing the end of his ballpoint pen. After a long and overly-dramatic pause, he asked, "Kevin, do you know why you're here today? I usually don't see you until Thursday. Why are you here on a Tuesday?"

Tyler could've answered honestly and said, "'Cause you all think I was trying to drown Sawyer in the cistern when really all I was trying to do was make him hear the water inside." He could've said that, the but rules for being a difficult kid meant making Dr. Cardenas work for it.

So Tyler farted.

"Kevin, please do not pass gas in my office," Dr. Cardenas said. "It's not very respectful."

Tyler chuckled. He was waiting until the stink hit Dr. Cardenas. He could tell when it happened. Dr. Cardenas was a very calm and proper person, but Tyler had had a deviled egg and some raisins for lunch so the smell was going to be extraordinary. Dr. Cardenas continued to talk, but Tyler had stopped listening. He was watching, waiting. Then Dr. Cardenas's nose twitched like someone had just stabbed him in the leg with a fork. There is was, Tyler grinned.

"That's not funny," Dr. Cardenas growled, stepping across the room to turn on his oscillating fan. "Why do you think that's funny? Do you think this is a funny situation?"

Tyler shrugged. "I don't think it's funny. I think it's stupid."

"What's stupid?"

"Being here is stupid. You all think I was trying to hurt Sawyer or something. But we were just playing. I was just showing him around his new home, being hospitable, you know? How was I to know that he doesn't like water. He has a phobia."

"A phobia, huh? How do you know that he has a phobia?"

"'Cause my foster mom told me he does. She said he gets upset about little things. She said he's 'highly-strung.'"

"Do you know what 'highly-strung' means?"

"It means he acts like a baby whenever something happens 'cause he's scared of stupid stuff. That's his phobia."

"So you think you're here because of Sawyer's phobias? Not because of your behavior?"

Tyler shrugged again. "I don't have no behavior. I told you, we were just playing."

"And his bad reaction to you playing around the cistern is because he has a phobia? A fear of water?"

Tyler nodded. "That's why he doesn't bathe."

"You've been thinking about this, I see."

34

"I've been thinking about it a lot. It's too bad he has his fear of water. I feel bad for him. Did you know that's called 'hydrophobia?'"

Dr. Cardenas raised his eyebrows. "That's right. The fear of water is called hydrophobia. But why do you think Sawyer has hydrophobia? Maybe he had a bad reaction because you were playing around a dangerous place where you weren't supposed to be."

"That's what I mean," Tyler frowned. "He was afraid of the cistern because it was full of water. That's why he doesn't bathe. That's why he's afraid of the ocean. That's why he doesn't like rain storms. It's all about his hydrophobia. But I didn't really know he had hydrophobia until he freaked out."

Tyler spent the next thirty-five minutes trying to convince Dr. Cardenas that the issue was really with Sawyer. Whether the adults wanted to see it or not, Tyler knew the eight-year-old boy was a mass of illogical fears. It was the longest conversation Tyler had ever had in that office and it was free of any additional bodily noises. But Tyler knew Dr. Cardenas wouldn't buy any of it. He never believed anything Tyler said unless it supported his own opinions.

Finally, Dr. Cardenas trotted out the same old questions he used every time Tyler landed in trouble. Fortunately, Tyler had ready-made answers for all of them.

"Kevin," Dr. Cardenas asked, "are you feeling jealous of this new boy being in your house?"

"Not really," Tyler answered truthfully, but then he saw the disappointed look on Dr. Cardenas's face and changed his answer. "Well, not so much anymore."

"You know," the doctor said, leaning back in his chair and picking at a fingernail, "it's normal for any child to feel a little threatened when someone new comes into the house."

"Yes, I was feeling insecure," Tyler said, demonstrating his excellent knowledge of the "special language" the adults in the child welfare system used. He knew insecurity was one of those concepts therapists loved. It was the grand excuse for anything bad anyone would ever do in their life... as long as you were a child. Tyler believed in using it frequently.

"Yes, yes," Dr. Cardenas agreed, looking more pleased. "You were insecure, weren't you? And why do you think you were insecure, Kevin?"

Different replies were popping through Tyler's head:

"Because you think my name is 'Kevin,' and I don't understand why I should take advice from someone who still doesn't know my name after seeing me every month for years."

Or:

"Because Sawyer smelled like a butt and I was sick of it."

Or:

"Because there's something up with Sawyer which no one seems to notice but me, something about all his phobias, and even though you don't believe about this, I'm gonna find out what it is..."

But Tyler finally settled with: "Because Karen and Griffin like him better than me."

Tyler didn't really believe what he said. After all, the little boy had been in the house for less than two weeks and he smelled like a butt most of that time. It was hardly a likable combination. But this excuse would quickly end the boring conversation with Dr. Cardenas. Karen might even take him out to a pizza dinner later to make him feel less insecure — it was the perfect plan!

For Tyler the simple truth was this: he lured Sawyer into the bathroom and sprayed him down with the super-soakers because the younger boy stank and it was a great opportunity to get him clean and have some fun too. And he took him to the cistern because it was old and weird and boys like old, weird things. But these reasons were too simple for the adults. They needed to

36

find layers of meaning behind everything Tyler did and so he tried to help them out whenever he could.

Dr. Cardenas scribbled in his chart:

"Kevin experienced an acute anxiety attack resulting from the introduction of a new child to the household which prompted him to lash out toward that child."

"Can I play with that fire truck?" Tyler asked him.

The doctor closed his folder and put down his pen. "There's no time for that today," he replied. "The next time you're in we'll make sure you get to play with the fire truck. Promise."

CHAPTER FOUR

As a result of the meetings with The Cowgirl and Dr. Cardenas, Karen now insisted Sawyer and Tyler play together only where she could see them — which further limited Tyler's plan to unlock the secret truth behind all of Sawyer's phobias.

Tyler had decided, after several days of observation, that Sawyer didn't have a complete fear of water as he first suspected. For example, the boy liked playing in rain puddles but hated thunderstorms. He didn't like the sound of crashing waves but helped wash the dishes in the kitchen sink every evening without any apprehension. In terms of keeping himself clean, Karen had convinced him to take sponge baths using the bathroom sink but he refused to go anywhere near the tub. When asked if he enjoyed swimming he answered firmly that he didn't know how to swim and had no interest in learning. He would stand for long periods of time and look at the ocean from the hilltop, but would steadfastly refuse to play on the beach. As strange as it seemed, Tyler knew there was some pattern to these fears which he alone had detected. He knew Karen would never believe him after recent events, so he decided to approach Griffin.

One evening, after Sawyer had gone to bed, Tyler climbed the twisted staircase up to Griffin's bedroom. The teenager was reorganizing his room to make space for the high-definition television he was certain he was going to receive on his impending birthday.

"Do you think I hate Sawyer?" he asked.

Griffin frowned and shrugged. "How would I know? You seem to have some kind of problem with him."

"Everyone says that but I really don't," Tyler insisted. "I like him. I like playing with him."

"Okay, then you tell me what's going on, Tyler. There have been lots of foster kids who have come in and out of this house in the time you've been here, but you've never been so weird around them as you are around Sawyer."

Tyler paused. He had the unfortunate trait of speaking without thinking, a trait that usually resulted in school suspensions and being confined to the house for days at a time. He was trying hard not to repeat those mistakes.

"He has secrets," Tyler said carefully.

Griffin snorted. "Is that it? You think he's keeping secrets so you have to figure out what they are? Maybe they're none of your business? Maybe you should butt out?"

"No, I mean he has really big secrets," Tyler said loudly. Louder than he meant to. Griffin set down the pile of books he was shifting and listened very carefully as Tyler explained his observations. This wasn't typical of him. Usually Tyler took little interest in the other kids who passed through the lighthouse. He knew they were temporary, so he made little effort to befriend them. Because of this, his interest in, and concern for, Sawyer was extraordinary.

When Tyler was finished, Griffin took a deep breath and replied, "That's all very interesting, but really all you've proven is that he's twitchy around water."

"Just water in certain ways," Tyler insisted. "Big amounts of water."

"Plenty of people have that, Tyler. Water can be scary. I think there's even a word for it. Aquaphobia? Marine-a-phobia? Something like that."

"It's called hydrophobia. Then there's the submarines."

"What submarines?"

"Sawyer's crazy about submarines, right? He talks about them, has all these crazy facts about them. I saw him building one out of Legos, right? Why is someone who's so scared of the water so interested in submarines?"

Griffin shrugged. "I don't know. Ask your shrink."

"People who are scared to fly in airplanes don't spend all their time building model airplanes, do they? If you're scared of something, why would you want to remind yourself of it? Submarines and water go together. The biggest water. The whole ocean."

Griffin scratched his nose and answered, "I'm not sure people who are scared to fly wouldn't build model airplanes, Tyler. Those are two different things altogether. I think sharks are pretty interesting fish, but I'm also scared of them. I certainly wouldn't go swimming with one although I love watching TV programs about them. I think you can be both interested in something and scared of it."

"Then I will prove it," Tyler said firmly. "I'll show you what I mean."

"Fine," Griffin chuckled. "Just don't use the bath tub or the cistern to prove it, okay?"

Griffin was just about to move a wooden bookcase when he stopped and looked over at Tyler.

"There's one other thing you need to think about," he said. Tyler could tell by the tone of Griffin's voice that this was serious. "You know what's happened to a lot of the kids who come through here, Tyler. You went through it yourself. You know how all of them were hurt and neglected. If you start putting your nose in Sawyer's business, if you start trying to find out his deep, dark secrets, you may bring up some stuff he's trying to forget."

A cold shiver ran up Tyler's spine. It had been nearly six years since he had been removed from his family's home. It had taken him four years to stop thinking of that day as being a bad thing, to stop thinking of the police officers who had bundled him out of there in a dirty blanket as being villains. And even after all this time, he still wasn't quite ready to call it a 'rescue,' although that's how Karen and Griffin always referred to it.

He had such mixed emotions about being a foster kid. In the front of his head, Tyler knew that Karen's lighthouse was a better place for him. It was warm and clean. There was always plenty of food. No one hit him or yelled at him or flicked burning cigarettes at him. But in the back of his head — way, way in back — he still missed his mother. He closed his eyes and tried to visualize her face. Her memory floated just out of reach, like a dream he could still feel but couldn't fully remember.

"I don't think Sawyer's secrets have anything to do with his, well, the stuff that happened to him," Tyler said.

Griffin snorted. "How do you know that?"

"I don't know," Tyler answered. "I just think this is about something else. Something that Sawyer doesn't even know about."

When Tyler went back to school on Monday, he exhibited four consecutive days of nearly perfect self-control. His teacher, who usually had a stack of referrals with his name on them printed up in advance, was so impressed by his behavior she made a special point to tell the principal about it. In turn, the principal caught Tyler in the hall and patted him softly on the shoulders.

"I'm so proud of how well you're doing this week, Tyler," the man said.

Tyler smiled weakly and thanked him for the compliment. He chose not to tell him that the reason for his good behavior was he wanted his library privileges on Friday so he could research his suspicions on Sawyer and somehow reveal a monumental secret which would shake up the entire Atlantic seaboard. This knowledge might've spoiled it for the principal.

When the end of the week rolled around, and Tyler had the library pass in hand, he went immediately to the computer catalog and began to search for anything related to submarines.

"Tyler, you're concentrating so hard here," Ms. Trease, the school librarian, said as she glanced over his shoulder. "No books on motorcycles and monster trucks this time, I see. Are you working on a research paper?"

For a moment, Tyler considered lying to her. He didn't know why exactly. Karen had always told him a person's reputation "walks in front of them." When people at the school saw Tyler's reputation walking down the hall, most would run and hide. This included many of the teachers. But Ms. Trease had always been a little different in that regard. Maybe it was because he didn't encounter her enough to actually annoy her? Or maybe she just didn't gossip about him the way many of the teachers did? Or maybe she was just genuine in her interest, something Tyler could sense just by looking past her big-rimmed glasses and into her soft hazel eyes?

Tyler shook his head. "It's personal research," he replied. "I need to find out if submarines ever had snorkels on them."

"Snorkels? Well, that's a very unusual topic."

"Yeah, someone I know told me that submarines used to have snorkels on them so the crews wouldn't suffocate because the insides of the submarines were filled with oil fumes. I'm trying to figure out if that's true."

"Wow. Well, let me show you where the books on boats and ships are. You should be able to find submarines in that area. They might have some pictures you can look at."

With Ms. Trease's help, Tyler ended up with a small pile of books and began to eagerly flip through the pages. His eyes scrutinized the grainy photographs and old illustrations of men in bellbottom trousers and cloth hats scrubbing decks and hoisting sails. He finally came to a large volume on the history of ocean warfare which contained an entire chapter on submarines, starting with the crude iron vessels used during the American Civil War and ending with modern nuclear powered warcraft. Hidden among these pages was one small black and white photo of a large pipe-like object cutting through the waves. The caption below the photo read: "Snorkels were used during the last years of the war to help recycle the air in submarines without requiring the boat to surface." On the opposite page were various photos of the cramped interior of a sub with men packed in shoulder-to-shoulder. Some were asleep, others were reading books or writing letters. The walls were lined with tubes and conduits and valves. Bare light bulbs threw the entire chamber into stark shadow, drawing heavy black lines across the young faces of the sailors. Their eyes looked lonely and afraid.

"Did you find what you were looking for?" Ms. Trease asked.

Tyler held up the book so she could see the photograph. "Snorkel," he said proudly. "But I don't know when this picture is from."

Ms. Trease balanced her glasses on the tip of her nose and skimmed the words on the page. "Oh, this is a picture of a German submarine. These subs were called U-boats," she said.

"When were they around?" Tyler asked.

"Oh, a very long time ago. U-boats don't exist anymore. But once they were very dangerous submarines used for war. Do you remember studying about World War Two in class?"

"Kind of, I guess."

"Well, that's when this photo was taken. It's a German U-boat during World War Two. If you want more on this, we can look in the section about this war."

An hour later, Tyler was able to leave the library with three books on the submarines of World War Two and several articles specifically on U-boats he'd printed off the Internet. Although he didn't enjoy reading, he spent the next two nights pouring through the pages and analyzing the photos. He had studied World War Two the previous year in school, but he couldn't remember any information about U-boats at all and was somewhat surprised to find what a horrifying impact they had made during the first few years of the war. Some of the books even went so far as to say the the U-boats almost won the war for the Germans. Almost.

As he read, images swirled through his head of entire cities on fire with smoke rising in columns so tall and thick it blotted out the sun. He envisioned the people of Great Britain, an island nation, stumbling through streets so disfigured by bomb craters it looked more like the surface of the moon. He imagined them digging through piles of rubble, struggling to find enough food to eat because the German U-boats were sinking all of the supply ships before they could deliver their cargo. He wondered what the U-boats must've looked like as they cut through the cold grey waves of the Atlantic Ocean in what were called "wolf packs" and the kind of terror a ship's crew must've felt when they saw them coming. Or worse, when they didn't suspect anything at all until a torpedo exploded against the hull. Tyler wondered exactly how many ships and people were lost in what became known as "The Battle of the Atlantic." The books gave estimates, but how could anyone know for sure? It was this final thought which bothered Tyler most, the thought of so many having died and no one even knowing where their bones now rested. He went to bed that night and dreamed of their ghosts wandering the dark and frigid ocean bottom, trapped forever in a memory of a war which had ended decades earlier.

To Tyler's disappointment, there was not a huge amount of information available on the use of snorkels on U-boats, although he was able to confirm they were constructed into new submarines during the last two years of the war because it became increasingly hazardous to surface due to enemy airplanes.

Now he decided it was time to test Sawyer's strange knowledge of submarines. It still made no sense to him how an eight-year-old would know so many unique details about subs when it had taken Tyler days to track down those same information with an entire library and the Internet at his disposal.

Sawyer was lying on the floor watching television. Tyler casually placed his stack of books and articles on the floor next to him.

"Look, I know you're interested in submarines," he said, "so I checked out some books from the library."

Sawyer propped himself up on one elbow and looked mildly interested. He reached out and dragged a book over, gingerly leafing through the pages. Then, to Tyler's annoyance, he closed the book and turned back to the television.

Tyler groaned quietly. He opened another book, found a page covered in photos of U-boats, and slid it next to the child. Twenty minutes went by without Sawyer noticing. Tyler waited, anxiously. Sawyer got up and went to the bathroom. He switched channels half a dozen times. He got a bowl of cereal, spilled it, cleaned up the mess and got another bowl of cereal. He went to the bathroom again. Then finally, upon his return, he spotted the photos and squatted down to inspect them.

He mumbled something to himself. It sounded like "uncle seat bottom."

"What?" Tyler asked.

Sawyer looked over at him, frowning. "Hmm?"

"You said something. What did you say?"

Sawyer shrugged. "I don't know. It's just my word."

"What word? Let me hear it."

"Underseaboat," Sawyer said softly, his fingers dancing over the photos of the submarines.

"What's that? What does that mean?" Tyler asked. He noticed that his heart was racing a little. Why was that?

"It's what I call submarines."

Tyler crawled onto the floor next to him and asked him about the boats in the photos. Sawyer's face brightened. He loved to explain things and spent the next ten minutes describing how periscopes worked, how the U-boats operated on batteries while underwater and diesel engines while surfaced. He explained how they could shoot torpedoes and sink other vessels from a great distance away.

Tyler's voice grew deep and somber. "How do you know all this, Sawyer?" he asked.

Sawyer shrugged. "I guess I just remember stuff," he replied before turning back to the television. The conversation was over, but Tyler had received what he needed.

That evening, he and Griffin jimmied open the broken padlock and snuck up to the very top of the lighthouse tower where they could be assured of complete privacy. There was no working electricity in this part of the house, so they carried flashlights and huddled together behind the giant, dusty lantern. Tyler laid out the books and other materials on the dirty floorboards. He was not very good at organizing his thoughts nor explaining himself, but he did the best he could and Griffin listened politely to every word.

"Okay, I still am not getting what you're thinking here," the older boy said, having tucked a flashlight under his chin as he leafed through one of the books. He paused to examine a colorful painting of a U-boat crew crammed onto a slippery deck. In the background, a plume of dark smoke was rising from a sinking ship.

Tyler felt frustrated. How can I explain something I don't totally understand himself, he wondered. "I'm saying that Sawyer doesn't just have an interest in U-boats. I'm saying that he's been on one," he replied.

Okay, that was clear and precise, Griffin thought. It also sounded completely nuts.

Griffin composed himself before he spoke. He didn't want to insult Tyler. He could see the boy was taking all of this very seriously. "Dude," he said, "these subs don't exist anymore. They were around in the 1930s and 40s. That was ages before Sawyer was even born."

"I don't know how to explain that part of it," Tyler said. "It's just a feeling I get. You should've been there when he was talking about them this afternoon. He knew all about how they work and fire torpedoes and stuff.

"That's something anyone could find out just by reading a website on the subject, Tyler.

"Yeah, but he even has his own special word for them: Underseaboats."

"What?"

"Underseaboats," Tyler repeated.

Griffin laughed. "'Under the sea boats?' That's what he's saying, Tyler. It's just a little kid's word."

"I don't think so."

"Well, how do you figure an eight-year-old ended up on submarines that don't exist anymore? He could've gone to a museum and seen one I guess? Do they have U-boat museums?"

"Yeah, they do," Tyler said, shuffling through his stack of papers. "Ms. Trease found one online and printed off the information for me. Here it is."

He handed several crumpled sheets to Griffin.

"Okay, maybe this's where he got his information?" Griffin suggested, running the flashlight beam quickly over the papers.

"Griffin, that museum's far away in Chicago. There's no way he could've been to it."

"Maybe he lived on a U-boat in a former life?" Griffin chuckled.

"Huh? What does that mean?"

"I was joking, Tyler."

"No, really, what did you mean?"

"Some people believe that we live many different lives and that we're different people in each life. Or sometimes we're animals. I guess it all depends. It's called reincarnation."

"That's weird. Do you think you've lived other lives?"

"Nah. I don't really believe in stuff like that. Plenty of people do, though."

"Do you think someone who was... what's it call?"

"Reincarnated."

"Right. Reincarnated. Do you think that someone who was reincarnated could actually remember a life they had lived before this one, before their current life?"

"I don't know, dude. I guess you could."

"So maybe what Sawyer's remembering are his own memories? Maybe he was a sailor on these subs in another life?"

Griffin was staring at the crumpled pages on the U-boat museum. A long, deep line ran across his brow.

"What? You think I'm stupid or something?" Tyler asked.

"Huh? No. What was that word Sawyer had for submarines? That baby word? Underwater boats?"

"Underseaboats," Tyler said. "Why? What's wrong?"

"Listen to this..." He began to read from the U-boat museum papers: "'The German World War Two Type-IXc Unterseeboot (submarine) was captured in battle by boarding parties from the USS Guadalcanal on June 4, 1944.' Dude, he didn't make up the word Unterseeboot... it's the German word for this type of submarine."

Tyler's head was clouded. "Sawyer speaks German?" he asked blankly.

"No," Griffin said, "but somehow he knows this word. Somehow he knows the German word for submarine."

CHAPTER FIVE

Over the next three days Tyler had no luck in getting Griffin to assist him with his investigation as the older boy was preoccupied with his impending birthday celebration. Conducting a successful nineteenth birthday party was not an easy trick for Griffin. He was no longer in high school but still living at home, so finding a way to have a more adult experience without your mother and young foster brothers cramping your style was requiring a great deal of tact. He and Karen had finally struck a deal. There would be a birthday party which would include the family on Saturday afternoon, after which Griffin and his friends would depart for a separate celebration outside of the home. Karen teased Griffin with threats of crepe paper decorations, pin-the-tail-on-the-donkey and clowns creating balloon animals, but the party was perfectly appropriate for young adults. For Tyler and Sawyer it was all very boring.

Griffin's guest list included former high school classmates and new acquaintances from his first year in junior college. For some reason Tyler couldn't quite understand, young women outnumbered young men by about two-to-one and they clustered in small groups and spoke in soft whispers and giggled a lot. Tyler felt completely invisible. Even the cat was more interesting to Griffin's friends as he occasionally solicited a scratch behind the ears.

Tyler noticed Griffin was particularly well groomed for the festivities. His jet black hair was spiked up to its maximum height and he'd even gone to the unusual length of ironing all his clothes. Tyler watched with amusement as he worked the room like a doctor works a trauma ward — bouncing from place to place, checking everyone's status before hurrying off again. He made it look effortless.

Upstairs, a special place had been prepared on the south wall for the 40-inch high-definition television he was certain Karen had purchased for him. But the afternoon's big surprise came when Karen disappeared for twenty minutes and then drove back up to the house in a blue sedan with the words HAPPY B-DAY GRIFF! written across the back window in white shoe polish. The car was used and had a paint job which was slightly faded and scratched, but the gift itself was completely unexpected. Griffin was speechless and even made the unusual gesture of hugging his mother in front of all his friends. The automobile was a little disheartening for Tyler. He knew it would mean seeing less of Griffin. It was another step toward the inevitable day when Griffin moved out and Tyler would truly be the oldest and longest-lasting boy in the lighthouse.

The following week, Tyler spent his after-school hours with Ms. Trease in the library. Ms. Trease found his new academic pursuits heartening, especially for a kid whose previous taste in literature included books on how to draw dinosaurs and magazines about professional wrestling. She didn't even bat an eye when he showed up and requested some books on reincarnation. While they browsed through the stacks and cruised the Internet together, she shared her afternoon snack of carrot sticks and ranch dressing. The experience made him feel almost normal. When he was working with Ms. Trease, he didn't feel like the trouble-maker kid who always had to sit right next to the teacher's desk or was always being sent to the principal's office. He just felt like Tyler.

To his surprise, the belief that human souls could be reborn in other bodies was very old and widespread across the world. For some major religions, like the Hindus and the Buddhists, reincarnation was an important motivation for living well. Both of those religions believed if you led a good and virtuous life today, you would be reborn into an even better existence the next time around. But the opposite was also true. If you were a mean and nasty person, you'd be reborn into a more lowly state, which might include coming back as something other than a human being. This idea of the quality of your life being linked to the your personal choices and actions was known as karma, with rebirth into a better life being the ultimate reward for good karma. Tyler paused to consider what he might come back as in a future life. It made him shudder.

With all the trouble I've been in over the years, it'll probably be something with six legs and antennae, he thought.

"Now here's something interesting," Ms. Trease said from behind her computer terminal.

"What's that?" Tyler asked.

"I found an article about a young girl who lived in Sri Lanka," she replied, pushing her large oval-shaped glasses to the tip of her nose. "When the girl was very young, she started telling stories about a previous life in which she had been a boy. She was able to describe this boy's family members, his house and was even able to remember which village he lived in. The girl's parents began to investigate her stories and eventually found a family whose son had died two years before their daughter was born."

Tyler walked over to Ms. Trease and peered over her shoulder at the monitor. Attached to the article was a grainy black and white photo of a tall, spindly woman standing next to a pretty girl in a white cotton dress. The girl appeared to be about ten-years old.

"Is that the little girl?" Tyler asked, pointing to the photo.

"Yes, and the woman with her is the mother of the boy who died earlier. Apparently the little girl was so convinced that this woman had been her mother in her previous life that she started calling her 'mama,'" Ms. Trease answered.

Tyler frowned. "How would you know if someone had your kid's soul in them?"

"The article says that the two sets of parents figured it out by testing the girl. They took some of the dead boy's old toys and clothes, mixed them up with a bunch of other stuff that had nothing to do with him, and then watched to see what the girl picked up and played with."

"Yeah, but that doesn't prove anything," Tyler said. "If they put one of the dead boy's toy guns in front of the girl, she probably wouldn't pick it up because girls really don't like to play with toy guns."

"Well, it seems like there was more to it than that. It had to be more than one object and a lot of it had to do with how the girl responded to the object."

"Like how?"

"In this case, the girl recognized the dead boy's belongings, identified them as her own and began to tell stories about how she used to play with them. The boy's parents confirmed that these stories were true."

Tyler was suddenly very aware of how hard his heart was beating in his chest.

"So reincarnated people could actually remember their past lives?" he asked.

"Or at least parts of their past lives," Ms. Trease said. "From the studies some scientists have done, it sounds like children are much more likely to remember past lives than adults. Apparently these past life memories fade with time. There also appears to be a trigger event in lots of cases."

"What does that mean?"

"Well, the reincarnated person may not have any memories of a past life until one day — boom — something unusual happens that triggers the memories. It might be hearing a particular piece of music, or visiting a new place, or even looking at an old photograph."

"So a kid with a reincarnated soul might be able to recognize places or objects from past lives just by looking at photos?"

"Maybe," Ms. Trease said, "But this article also says that the child may not understand why they recognize or are drawn to certain items or places. They are interested in them but can't explain where their interest comes from."

"And how did these parents know where to look for their daughter's former life?"

"Well, in her case she actually remembered the village that the dead boy lived in. However, the studies suggest that a soul doesn't travel very far from the site of death. Usually not any further than a hundred miles."

Tyler went home that evening preoccupied with thoughts about Sawyer, past lives, karma, German submarines and how they all connected together. Like the Sri Lankan parents searching for their daughter's former life as a boy, Tyler had inadvertently tested Sawyer's knowledge of past events by showing him the photos of U-boats. But in the end, it didn't prove anything except that Sawyer was interested in World War II submarines and had a good deal of knowledge about them. In order to prove that Sawyer's knowledge came from a past life experience, he'd have to do something more... he'd have to find the body Sawyer's soul had once occupied.

The holding cell had yellow plaster walls and an iron door which screamed with rust and old age every time it swung open. A single light bulb hung from the ceiling, snapping and popping with electricity. Ehren had been sitting in the cell so long he was beginning to see pictures in the cracked plaster... a deer... a leafless tree... the face of an old man. He squinted. The face could have been his father's with its deep crevices and sad eyes. He wondered how his parents were. There was no way of knowing if they were even still alive. The Allied bombing raids over his country had flattened entire cities. The Nazis were losing the war, but they didn't have the good sense to surrender.

Hitler will ruin us forever before this is over, he thought. He'll fight the Americans and the British to the last man... and when it's over there will be no one left to rebuild the country.

He glanced up at the ceiling where the light bulb flickered and crackled. He tried to determine where the microphones were hidden, but the Americans had disguised them too well.

Another U-boat had been captured, the American naval officers had told him. Time to dress in your prisoner of war clothes and sit in the holding cell. Remember to speak up this time, they admonished him. The microphone's powerful, but we still can't hear if you whisper.

Over the last few months, Ehren had become an effective intelligence tool for the Americans. Armed with a fake name and the authenticity of being a genuine German submariner, he'd been able to coax information out of new P.O.W.s in a way no American could. He put them at ease with his big smile and willingness to gossip. The new prisoners would tell him everything from battle plans to the types of submarines now being used during Germany's final hour of the war. Most of the men he spoke with felt Germany's defeat was just months away and this helped loosen their tongues. He figured they didn't care to keep secrets when they were doomed anyway.

Lieutenant Spolarich and Major Sharpe had promised Ehren a permanent home in the United States after the war. They would find his parents and bring them over as well. They told him he could make a good life in the States. He was young and strong and spoke excellent English. Plus, the naval officers reminded him, he would never be able to return to Germany. Even those countrymen who hated the Nazis would consider him a traitor. He looked at the cracked plaster wall and squinted his eyes again. The face of the old man stared back.

Am I a traitor? he asked himself. He couldn't see it that way. To him there was a greater good to be won. It wasn't so much that he needed the Americans to win the war. He needed the Nazis to lose. He needed to know that Germany after the war would not include bonfires piled with outlawed books; or massive rallies which celebrated a mythical "master race;" or trains stuffed with Jews destined for concentration camps. He needed to know that Germany after the war wouldn't be a place where your parents were abducted only to return a year later crippled and broken. He needed to know that post-war Germany would not be Nazi Germany.

He heard the outer doors bang open and the shuffling of dozens of feet against the cement floor. The new P.O.W.s had arrived.

Remember to speak up, he told himself, so the microphones can hear you.

On Saturday morning, the Cowgirl showed up at the house again. From experience, Tyler's first reaction was to think about what he'd done to prompt her visit, and finding nothing he began to panic. Then he saw who was with her. A young man and woman stepped out of the back seat of her car. They were wearing very nice clothes, the type you'd expect someone to wear to a fancy party or a college graduation, but certainly not for visiting a house full of unruly boys. The Cowgirl opened the car's trunk and the young woman reached inside and pulled out a large gift bag festooned with curled ribbon. Tyler immediately knew who they were: new foster parents.

Karen's lighthouse was generally considered a temporary home for the boys who lived there, and eventually all of them moved onto other places. As such, it wasn't unusual for visiting foster parents to show up with the caseworkers — usually carrying gift bags or packages in festive wrapping paper — for that first, awkward visit with their prospective child. Tyler knew instinctively this couple in their beautiful clothes and carrying their offerings of toys and candy were for Sawyer. No one new had shown up to meet Tyler in over a year and he'd given up expecting it.

He ran off to find Sawyer, but the younger boy was already downstairs and giddy with expectation. Meeting new parents created the possibility for something close to a normal life and Tyler couldn't fault him for his excitement. For foster kids, permanency was more precious than money, toys or even a later bedtime.

The Cowgirl knelt down so she could look Sawyer eye-to-eye and said, "Sawyer, do you remember the nice people I told you I was bringing for a visit? Well, this is Lane and Tracy. They're brand new foster parents and they're looking for a special little boy just like you."

Immediately Sawyer's interrogation of the prospective parents began:

"Do you have a big house? Do you have a dog? Am I allowed to play with the dog? Does the dog have bad breath? Did you know that you can brush a dog's teeth? Do you have cable television or a satellite dish? Will I have to share my room with anyone? Can the dog sleep in my room?"

Tyler put his hand over Sawyer's busy mouth and said, "He's just a little hyper today. He talks a lot."

The woman, Tracy, looked a little confused and replied, "Oh, that's okay. We like questions. We have a lot of questions ourselves."

Karen pried Tyler's hand off of Sawyer's mouth and coaxed him away with a firm grip on his shoulder. "This's my son, Tyler," she said. "But, Tyler, I think we can let Sawyer express himself right now. Why don't you folks go into the living room and make yourselves at home. You can have a nice long chat."

"I'll show you!" Tyler yelled, wiggling out from underneath Karen's fingers and bounding over to the couch. The others followed, but warily. "Sawyer, you can sit next to me and open your gifts."

Sawyer climbed obediently onto the couch next to Tyler. Lane and Tracy sat in armchairs across from them. Karen and the Cowgirl exchanged meaningful looks.

"Tyler," Karen said kindly, "why don't we let Lane and Tracy and Sawyer get to know each other? Why don't you come and help me in the kitchen for a while?"

"No thanks," Tyler said quickly.

"Tyler..." Karen said, more firmly now.

"Yup?"

"We really want to give Lane, Tracy and Sawyer some time together alone."

"I won't get in the way."

"Please come into the kitchen with me."

"I said I won't get in the way."

"You are getting in the way and you need to come into the kitchen now." Karen's cheeks had darkened and her eyes were wide. Tyler glanced around the room. All of the adults were staring at him. Screwed up again, he told himself. Never doing the right thing at the right time or in the right place.

Without a word he slid off the couch and plodded into the kitchen. As soon as he was out of sight, Sawyer's line of rapid-fire questions continued followed by laughter, the tearing and crumpling of wrapping paper and shrieks of delight. Phineas the cat was sitting in a puddle of sunlight on the kitchen table. He glanced up at Tyler and began to purr. Tyler stroked the animal's ears. They were soft like a velvet ribbon. Somehow, he thought, Phineas had this whole thing right... ignore everyone and don't worry about their feelings, and then when you want attention wriggle your way onto a warm lap and refuse to leave until you've received so much petting you can't take anymore.

Karen came in a moment later and patted Tyler on the back. She meant it kindly but it felt condescending to him.

"That was nice of you to let them have their time together," Karen said as she began to load some dirty cups into the dishwasher.

"It wasn't nice of me," Tyler replied. "You made me leave."

"It was nice that you did as I asked without making a big fuss. This's a wonderful opportunity for Sawyer, you know?"

"I know."

"It could mean a brand new home for him with brand new parents."

"I know, Karen, I get it," Tyler said.

She paused and looked at him. "Are you upset by their visit?"

Tyler shrugged and tickled Phineas's chin. The cat lifted his head and closed his eyes. He purred louder. "No one will ever come to see me, will they?" he asked.

"I don't know," Karen replied gently. "You can never really know for sure. One day, someone may come forward and say, hey, that Tyler kid is just who I'm looking for. He's the one who will make my family just perfect. But, until that day comes, you are now and forever part of our family."

Tyler snorted. "Yeah," he said, "I'm a piece of furniture."

"Huh? What does that mean?"

"I'm part of the family like furniture is part of a family. Like a sofa. You keep it a really long time until it's too old and then it goes out the door and you forget about it."

Karen looked shocked. She hadn't realized Tyler felt this way. He was very skilled at ignoring his own feelings, as if he denied his emotions long enough he'd cease to have them altogether.

Before she could respond, Tyler pushed open the back door and ran out into the yard. He rounded the house and crawled back under the boxwood bushes and closed his eyes. When he opened them again, the sun was down and there were footsteps on the wooden planks of the front porch. Tracy, Lane and the Cowgirl were saying goodbye to Sawyer. He was excitedly thanking them for his gifts and asking when he'd see them again. Soon, they promised. The front door closed and the adults paused for a moment on the lawn, about six feet from where Tyler was hidden.

"So, what do you think?" the Cowgirl asked.

"He's wonderful. Such a charming little guy," Tracy gushed.

"Yeah," Lane replied, "we definitely want to pursue this. I think he's the child for us."

CHAPTER SIX

That evening, Griffin knocked at Tyler's door. It was rare that he came to the younger boys' rooms, complaining they smelled too much like dirty feet. Tyler was lying on the bed, scribbling in a spiral notebook with a ballpoint pen.

"Hey," he smiled. "Can I come in?"

Tyler waved him in and Griffin quietly closed the door behind him.

"I thought I'd come by and see how your little investigation was going," he whispered. "Have you found out anything new?"

Tyler was unimpressed with the older boy's sudden interest. "Do you really care?" he asked. "You haven't cared since you got your car."

Griffin bit his lip. "Sorry 'bout that, man. You'll understand when you get your first ride. It's kind of exciting, y'know? But I didn't mean to blow you off or anything. I've just been a little distracted."

"Yeah, okay."

"Really. I mean it."

"Okay. We're cool."

"Okay, so fill me in..."

Tyler pulled the notebook higher so it blocked his face and kept scribbling without saying a word.

Griffin tried again. "Mom told me what you said to her today. You don't really feel like a piece of furniture here, do you?"

"Are you in here because you really want to know about my investigation or because you just feel guilty or something?" Tyler asked.

"I don't feel guilty, dude. I don't have anything to feel guilty about. I just don't want you to feel that way because we don't feel that way about you. You may be here as a foster child, Tyler, but that doesn't mean that Mom and I don't think of you as family."

Tyler dropped the notebook. He felt his eyes beginning to sting with tears. "But I'm not family, Griff. I'm not adopted here. If someone came by tomorrow and wanted to adopt me, you and Karen would wave goodbye to me at the door and then we'd never see each other again. That's how it works, right? Foster families are just temporary."

"Maybe the situation's temporary while you're waiting for something permanent to come along, but that doesn't mean we'd stop thinking about you if you were adopted tomorrow. I'd hope that we would still see each other, y'know, hang out and stuff. Even when you become an adult, I'd hope that would be the case because I've always thought of you as both my brother and my friend."

"Really? How many of the other kids who have come through here do you still see and hang out with, Griffin? I'll tell you how many — none. Because they come and go and that's how it is."

Griffin swallowed hard. "Most of those kids were only here for a few weeks, Tyler... And none of them were you. For whatever reason, you came and stayed. We like having you here and nobody wants to see you go."

Tyler put the notebook over his face to hide his tears. It was the cruel irony of his life that he came into the foster system because he lost his family, and then cycled endlessly through other families while he hoped to eventually find a permanent situation. But the fact was, no matter what kind of happy face the Cowgirl or Karen put on it, Tyler knew he was going to be one of those foster kids who never got adopted. The next few years would just be a waiting game until he turned eighteen and started his adult life with no more roots than he had during his childhood. He felt stuck between two lives — the one he once had and the one he'd been promised but had yet to receive.

"Griffin," he choked, his body shuddering, "I don't remember what my mom looks like."

Griffin stood there for a long time, at a complete loss on how to respond to that statement. His parents had divorced and his father now lived out of state, but he spoke to him, visited with him during the summers, sent emails and traded photographs. It was difficult for Griffin to imagine what it would be like to have no mementos of your parents, and to find that over time even the memories you clung to were becoming hazy and unreliable. And in that moment, standing over a sobbing thirteen-year-old boy, Griffin felt something which didn't come easily to any teenager: he felt bad for Tyler.

Thank god the door's closed, he said to himself as he sat down on the edge of the bed and wrapped his arms awkwardly around the boy's shoulders. Tyler convulsed silently, his face buried against Griffin's left arm. Griffin began to wonder how long he had to hold the kid? What was the appropriate time so Tyler understood his sincerity but Griffin didn't wind up with a shirt soaked with tears and snot? After two or three minutes, Tyler pulled away and looked up at Griffin with red eyes.

"You hugged me, dude," he said.

"Yeah, it's no biggie, right?" Griffin asked.

"No. No biggie. It was okay. Thanks."

"Sure." Griffin paused, standing up and taking a few steps away. "I meant what I said, Tyler. I wouldn't lie to you about that stuff. You're my brother in spirit if not in blood, okay?"

"Okay."

Griffin smiled. "Now, update me on your investigation."

Tyler had done a huge amount of reading about paranormal phenomena and briefed Griffin on what he referred to as "the four major rules of reincarnation" which were neatly written out in his notebook:

A soul can be reincarnated anywhere from a few days to decades after the death of the original body. When you come back depends on why you need to come back. There's usually some purpose, some new lesson to be learned.

The soul usually doesn't travel any further than one hundred miles from the site of death before it's reborn into a new body.

The soul may remember its former life, but these memories usually fade with time and are gone by the time the person's an adult.

Your fears, interests and habits may be effected to some extent by your past life... but you may not realize it.

Griffin blinked with amazement and asked, "Did you make that stuff up?"

"No," Tyler insisted. "Real scientists have been researching this stuff for years and years. There's this organization in England called the Society for Psychical Research. It was formed over a hundred years ago and they've been researching ghosts and reincarnation and stuff like that ever since. They're all scientists and really smart people. They have thousands of case studies on it."

"And what did they decide?"

"I don't know if they really decided anything. It's kind of a hard thing to prove, even though they have lots of cases where they just can't explain what happened."

"But you think all this stuff is real? You think Sawyer was reincarnated from some German sailor?"

"Submariner."

"What?"

"If the sailor works on a submarine, he's called a submariner."

"What a smarty! Fine... you think Sawyer was reincarnated from some German submariner?"

"Yes. And I think I have a way of proving it."

"Okay. I'm really interested in how you're going to connect Sawyer to a German U-boat."

"One of the rules of reincarnation is that when you die, your soul usually doesn't travel any further than one hundred miles, right? If we can find out where Sawyer was born, then we can find out if it was in a hundred miles of where a U-boat was sunk."

Griffin sighed. "Tyler, think about this carefully," he said. "I think it's safe to say that Sawyer was born in the United States somewhere. Not too many U-boats were sunk around here, I think."

Tyler laughed. "That's where you're wrong!" he said. He dug out one of the library books Ms. Trease had found for him and cracked the pages open. He laid it flat on the bed and pointed. It was a map of the eastern coastline of the United States from Maine to Florida. Various stars and dots followed the coast, indicating where U-boat activity had taken place between the years of 1939 and 1944. Surprisingly, many of the locations were relatively close to Karen's lighthouse.

"Wow," Griffin responded, genuinely impressed. "Atlantic City, Cape Hatteras, Chesapeake Bay, Cape Cod! It's amazing that these subs got this close to our shores."

"That's what they were made for... to be sneaky. There are even some famous cases where a U-boat snuck into an enemy harbor, sunk a bunch of ships and then snuck back out again without anyone catching them. Look at the next page."

Griffin flipped the map and inspected a rather blurry photo of twinkling cityscape. It was nighttime and the skyscrapers were lit up like Christmas trees, their glowing windows reflected in the swirling ocean waters below.

"That looks like New York City," Griffin said.

"It is New York City," Tyler grinned. "That photo was taken by a U-boat captain through his periscope before Germany and the United States were at war. After the war started, all the cities on the coast had to black out their lights because they were afraid the Germans would bomb them. But before the U.S. went to war, this U-boat captain snuck into New York harbor close enough to take this photo. Once the war began, the U.S. Navy was always fighting U-boats right off the coast. The submarines were trying to sink all the supply vessels sailing to England. So, if there was that much U-boat stuff going on right off shore, it's possible that one of those submariner's souls could've been reborn years later in a little American boy."

Griffin snorted. "Man, does this sound nuts," he grumbled. "But how are you going to prove this?"

"First things first," Tyler said confidently. "You need to find out where Sawyer was born."

"Me? Why me?"

"Because Karen always keeps all the foster kids' records locked up and I'd never be able to see them. But you can do it."

Griffin begrudgingly agreed, and later that night, after Karen had gone to bed, he snuck quietly into her study, unlocked her filing cabinet and read Sawyer's case history. Like so many of the boys who wandered in and out of the lighthouse, his file was filled with great sadness and suffering, but there was nothing in it to support the notion of reincarnation. His task completed, Griffin called Tyler to his room to report his findings.

"Baltimore," he said. "Sawyer was born in Baltimore and then his mother and father moved here when he was four."

Tyler's mind was racing. "Okay, so we need to see if any U-boats were sunk near Baltimore. Where's Baltimore?"

"In Maryland. That's about three hundred miles to the south of us."

"Is it on the ocean?"

"Yeah, it's on Chesapeake Bay."

"Chesapeake Bay was one of the areas where there was U-boat activity!" Tyler said. His heart was pounding with excitement.

"That doesn't mean a U-boat was sunk there, Tyler."

"But if one was, I'll find it," Tyler promised.

Ehren was escorted out of the military compound by Lieutenant Spolarich and another naval officer whom he'd never met before. Both men had changed out of their uniforms and were dressed in neatly pressed jackets and thin ties. They'd given Ehren new clothes as well, including leather shoes, a fedora hat and a wool overcoat to protect him from the falling snow.

The buildings and trees outside were frosted white and glistened in the lights from the surrounding buildings. A dark-colored car was waiting in the driveway in front of the main barracks, its engine idling and puffs of exhaust floating from its tailpipe. The officers had hidden it behind a cluster of trees and shrubs so no prisoner-of-war in the surrounding buildings could see who was being escorted out. Ever since Ehren had agreed to help the Americans, they'd treated him better. He was quickly removed from the general population of incoming P.O.W.s, many of whom were housed in a muddy "tent city," and was given private quarters in an entirely different building. Although still under lock and key, he enjoyed a ceiling over his head which didn't leak every time it rained and had certain basic privileges the other prisoners lacked. He was provided with an old radio and was allowed to listen to music and even the nightly news. Lieutenant Spolarich, who knew he was artistic, had purchased him a sketch book and some color pastels. He was given civilian clothes, although he had to change back into his khaki P.O.W. uniform whenever he was placed into the holding cell with the microphones. The Americans even gave him a fake name — Heinrich Offermann — which he used whenever new prisoners arrived. All of this was intended to protect and preserve the Americans' most valuable intelligence tool.

He was also given a title of sorts, a term that the Americans had for Germans like him: stool-pigeon. He liked the term better than traitor, but it wasn't meant as a compliment. Most of the Americans he worked with, with the exception of Lieutenant Spolarich, disdained him. A stool pigeon was someone who was valuable, but rarely respected.

As the months dragged on, the war news had grown increasingly bad for the Germans and the other Axis nations. The Americans, British, French and Canadians had invaded the European mainland and were liberating city after city from German control. Entire German armies were being wiped out or were surrendering. And for other submariners? Ehren cringed at the thought of it. Life was guaranteed to be short for the poor soul serving on a U-boat!

More and more prisoners were now being funneled through the American military post Ehren called home. He was sent to work in the bugged holding cell nearly every day. If there was a P.O.W. who was particularly valuable or hard to crack, then the

Americans would make sure Ehren became the man's roommate for a while. And when there were no prisoners to gossip with, Ehren spent his time translating intercepted communications for Lieutenant Spolarich.

The lieutenant had come to like Ehren and had recently become concerned for the young man's safety. The P.O.W. camps in the western United States were filling up and arriving prisoners at the fort were not moving out as quickly as before. As a result, some of the German detainees were beginning to compare notes about the chatty "Heinrich Offermann" who mysteriously showed up with every new batch of captives and then vanished just as mysteriously. He was clearly a native German, but he was too curious, too eager to talk about ship movements and recent battles. These were all things German sailors were taught never to speak about.

Lieutenant Spolarich had actually gone to Major Sharpe's office earlier in the week and had suggested it might be time to "retire" their favorite stool pigeon and move Ehren to another facility where he could remain safely anonymous. Major Sharpe had rebuffed the suggestion, however, reminding Spolarich that war had risk, even in P.O.W. camps.

But tonight, neither Ehren nor Lieutenant Spolarich wanted to worry about the tense whispers circulating among the other prisoners. Ehren was bundled into the car and they roared down the wide boulevard toward the fort's main gate. As they passed the chapel, a long rectangular building with a whitewashed spire, Ehren could hear faint hymnal music rising through the icy air. The stained glass windows were aglow, speckling the snow outside with patches of red, blue, yellow and orange. The snow glistening on the eaves and window ledges reminded him of the silvery decorations he used to string on the Christmas tree every year as a boy. The car hurried on, out the fort's main gate and winding its way through the city of Baltimore, passed quaint wooden homes dripping with icicles and *shops decorated with twinkling lights and holiday garlands.*

"Do you know what tonight is?" Lieutenant Spolarich asked Ehren.

Ehren knew. He was very careful to track his days in captivity. Every day that passed was a day closer to the war's end. "It's Christmas Eve," he beamed.

"Right," the lieutenant nodded. "So consider this my Christmas gift to you."

The car pulled to the curb and the men stepped out into a large city square. A fifteen-foot Christmas tree, strung with blue, green and red light bulbs shimmered across the street. Hundreds of American shoppers were bustling around, carrying packages or walking arm-in-arm for warmth.

"Do us a favor, Mr. Tschantz," Lieutenant Spolarich whispered. "Don't talk unless you have to. Your English is very good, but you can't hide that accent of yours."

Ehren nodded and followed obediently as they led him over to the cinema. The theater's marquee read OLD ACQUAINTANCE in large black letters. Lieutenant Spolarich had felt a little guilty taking the young German to a campy comedy which was widely billed as a "woman's film." Unfortunately, there weren't many choices as so many of the movies being produced had war themes and were decidedly anti-German. It didn't seem right to take Ehren to a film like that. Not as a reward; and certainly not on Christmas Eve.

To the lieutenant's relief, Ehren was delighted that the film featured Bette Davis, one of Hollywood's most famous actresses, and didn't seem to care much about the plot at all. The three men entered the theater quietly and sat at the back, away from the other patrons. Ehren trembled with excitement as the theater lights dimmed and the music intensified. He hadn't told Lieutenant Spolarich that he'd only been to a theater once before, when he was taken by his mother as a teenager. But motion pictures in Nazi Germany were a very different experience from those in the United States. Most were either heavily censored by the government or the story was infused with subtle messages planted there by the Nazis. Ehren's father had eventually forbade him from going to the movies, saying they were only mindless propaganda meant to turn Germans into obedient, unthinking servants. Instead, his mother and father provided him with musical instruments, art supplies and a variety of books, most of which were outlawed or would've been frowned upon by his teachers and friends. He remembered how much it pained his parents, both of whom were intelligent and highly-educated, that reading the wrong book could land you in jail.

Ehren had to wonder if a film such as OLD ACQUAINTANCE would've ever been allowed to play in his hometown. He doubted that a movie about two ambitious, career-minded women would've sat well in Hitler's Germany, where women were all expected to be mothers to the next generation of soldiers. He thought about his own mother, who had a college education but who didn't work outside the home for fear of being perceived as different. Intelligent people were often seen as a threat by the Nazis, so after his father was imprisoned his mother took great care to hide her own intellectualism. Still, late at night, she'd sit on the edge of Ehren's bed and read to him from the classics. His favorites were The Three Musketeers and The Vicomte of Bragelonne, both by a French author named Alexandre Dumas. Both were adventure stories where good-hearted people defeated powerful villains. If he ever made it to France, he promised himself to seek out all the famous places where those novels were set.

Sitting there in the darkness, Ehren forgot for a while about his predicament. Instead he thrilled at the sight of Bette Davis with her large, evocative eyes and the sound of her husky voice. He marveled at the glamor and opulence of New York City, a metropolis he'd often *imagined as being quite like Paris with its towering buildings and gleaming lights. He laughed at the melodramatic antics of the heroines although he had difficulty understanding their rapidly spoken English. For a while, he forgot about the war, about his parents, about his homeland in ruins. He even forgot about the the lieutenant's warnings of the increasing danger he was in among the other German sailors.*

   Tyler and Griffin had spent nearly a week conspiring on how they'd manage to drive to Baltimore, Maryland, without Karen finding out and Sawyer refusing to cooperate. Neither of them expected Sawyer to go willingly. A boy his age wouldn't see an eight-hour round trip as being a pleasant thing, especially when they were unable to tell him where they were going and why. It became obvious to Tyler that they'd have to bribe him. And it became even more obvious that what Sawyer expected in return for his cooperation was an afternoon at Freddy Puffenagle's Pizza Emporium.
   Freddy Puffenagle's Pizza Emporium was the most popular destination point in town for children between the ages of 3 and 8, but for Tyler and nearly everyone else it was something to be endured for the occasional birthday party or consolation lunch when a child's pee-wee soccer team failed to make the playoffs. The restaurant had mediocre food which consisted mostly of bland, cardboard-like pizza, a messy salad bar and baskets of greasy buffalo wings. Tyler remembered when he was younger and the arcade games, plastic ball pits and the intricate system of suspended tubes where he could crawl, hide and occasionally throw up actually seemed like fun. But that was then. Now he just thought

the whole place smelled of tomato sauce and sweaty children.

He and Griffin agreed to take Sawyer to Freddy Puffenagle's Pizza Emporium for four hours, let him gorge on pizza and all-you-can-drink soda pop and give him an unlimited supply of arcade tokens; and in return he'd accompany them on their secretive road trip to Maryland. It was a painful arrangement for the older boys but Tyler knew he'd have to tough it out, and he even degraded himself by performing the "Chicken Dance" with Sawyer and a costumed penguin named "Partytime Percy." The experience seemed to satisfy Sawyer and the following Saturday they were ready for the long car ride. Griffin told Karen he was going to take the boys to a large state park for a day of playing frisbee and picnicking. Karen was pleasantly surprised by his renewed interest in Tyler and Sawyer and decided to spend the day soaking in a mud bath at a day spa.

Despite his help, Tyler knew Griffin didn't think the trip would accomplish anything. Over the last few days, they'd spent a lot of time on the internet researching U-boat activity along the Atlantic seaboard and the Maryland coast in particular. Several submarines had been attacked and sunk by American ships in the area, but even Tyler had to confess he didn't know which of these boats might've contained the nameless, faceless man they were searching for. The books he'd consulted on reincarnation experiences had plenty of examples of people who spontaneously remembered past lives when confronted with a place they had once lived, but was it reasonable to assume Sawyer would have that same type of experience just by visiting the area? Besides, Griffin pointed out, if Sawyer was a submariner who had been killed off the Maryland coast decades earlier, he wouldn't have seen Maryland itself. Still, Tyler was insistent they were on the right path and he continued to search the internet right up until the morning of their departure. His hard work had paid off, as he had located several museums and military facilities with information on the U-boat war. Their first two stops proved useless however. Their final stop to was at Fort George G. Meade, a large military installation in the center of Baltimore.

The fort wasn't anything like Tyler had imagined. It was a self-contained community complete with stately residential neighborhoods and wide tree-lined streets. Since its establishment nearly one hundred years earlier, Tyler imagined the base had been through many transformations. He tried to discern which building or street or monument might've stood there during the Second World War. They passed a towering church with a white steeple. Tyler turned and gazed at the building through the car's back window. It reminded him of a medieval castle. All it needed was a drawbridge and armored men on horseback.

The military museum was a large white building with a peaked roof surrounded by grassy fields and what appeared, at first glance, an antique arsenal. A missile twice the height of the museum sat on the front lawn; and a neat line of old tanks and armored personnel vehicles was assembled nearby, causing Sawyer to coo with adoration.

"Oh!" the child cried. "Can we play on them?"

His question was clearly rhetorical, for he'd let himself out of the car and was running over to the immense steel vehicles before Griffin could even shut off the engine. The older boys allowed him play for a while, knowing the trip had been longer and more boring than they had promised.

After about twenty minutes, they were able to coax him over to the museum entrance. Tyler stood at the doorway and suddenly felt very disheartened. The displays inside were extensive and complex.

Griffin had the same reaction. "Dude," he whispered to Tyler, "this place is huge. We could be here all day and never find anything... and we don't have that kind of time."

"I don't like how it smells," Sawyer offered. "It makes my nose itchy."

There was a old African-American man sitting at a desk nearby. He looked to be in his seventies with close-cropped white hair and a neatly groomed mustache. "It's free to come in if that's what you boys are worrying about," he called cheerfully.

Griffin cleared his throat and walked across to the desk. "Is this the war museum?" he asked.

"Of course." The old man chuckled and said, "Couldn't you tell from all the hardware out on the front lawn?"

"Do you get to drive those tanks?" Sawyer asked.

The man laughed again and shook his head. "No, my man, those tanks don't work anymore. They're just for display." He leaned close to Sawyer and whispered, "When some things get old, they don't work as well as they used to."

"You're old but you still work," Tyler said.

Griffin slapped him on the shoulder. "Dude, don't talk to people like that."

Tyler suddenly felt embarrassed. He meant it as a compliment. But the old man didn't seem to mind and laughed again. "So," he said, "what brings you young men out to our little museum on a beautiful Saturday morning? This doesn't seem like a place where you'd normally spend a day off from school."

"Actually, I made them come with me," Griffin said. "I'm doing research on the U-boat war during World War II for a school paper. I was hoping you might have some materials on that."

"Well you certainly came to the right place, my friend," the man said. He rose from his chair and motioned for them to follow. "Let me show you something."

He led them into the grassy courtyard just outside the museum's entrance. He gestured broadly to the tree-lined horizon and the various buildings which surrounded them. "During the Second World War, this was one of the first places where Germans captured off of U-boats would come. Some of these buildings were used as dormitories to house prisoners of war while they were being interviewed and processed. They'd stay here for a week or two, and then they'd put them on trains and ship them west to prisoner-of-war camps."

"So Germans actually lived here?" Tyler asked, as he pulled his digital camera from his front pocket and began to snap photos of the surrounding buildings.

The old man nodded. "You bet. When crews were captured or rescued off of German vessels, our boys would bring them here as prisoners."

Tyler and Griffin exchanged glances. Suddenly, Tyler felt that his theory of the German submariner seemed more possible. During all his research and discussions with Griffin, he'd never thought about prisoners-of-war from U-boats.

"How do you capture someone off a submarine?" Tyler asked. "Wouldn't you just sink it and everyone inside would die?"

"Most of the time, that was probably the case," the old man said, leading them back inside and through a maze of exhibition halls. He stopped in front of a large display case filled with photographs and newspaper clippings. A neatly-painted sign read THE U-BOAT WAR ALONG THE AMERICAN COAST. Toward the center of the display were several photos obviously snapped from an airplane during an attack on a U-boat. The photo series clearly depicted the spray from bullets and depth-charges hitting the water around the submarine; the crew members jumping into the waves as they abandoned the stricken vessel; and finally the sinking of the smoking hulk itself.

"You see, during this war submarines weren't as advanced as they are now," the old man explained. "They had two types of engines. Diesel engines if the boat was traveling along the surface of the water, and batteries for when the boat was submerged. The problem was, the batteries only lasted a few hours and then you have to surface to recharge them. You also had to surface from time to time to let fresh air in, or you know what would happen?"

"The men would all suffocate?" Sawyer said brightly.

"That's right," the old man replied, impressed. "While under the water, the crew is using up all the oxygen in the sub. Eventually the U-boat captain would have to surface the boat to take on fresh air and power up those batteries. But if our guys found a U-boat on the surface, they'd attack it and hope to sink it. Most of the time the crews were trapped inside and would die. Sometimes, however, like in these photos, the crew members might be able to escape and jump into the ocean where they might be rescued."

"And then they came here?" Griffin asked.

"Well, there were several bases along the east coast that housed prisoners-of-war, but Fort Meade kind of specialized in submariners."

Tyler was feeling impatient. "Did any of them die here?" he said bluntly.

The old man raised an eyebrow. "Oh, yes, of course. Some of the men rescued off the U-boats would be injured or sick. There was a hospital here, but of course you'd expect that some of them might die. Or maybe some of them would try to escape and the guards would shoot them. We actually have a very famous prisoner-o-war buried in the graveyard here."

Griffin was suddenly interested. "Who was that?" he asked.

"Werner Henke. Ever heard of him?"

Griffin shook his head.

"He was shot while trying to escape from Fort Hunt in Virginia. But he's buried here. He was a very famous U-boat captain."

"U-boats?" Tyler exclaimed. "He was off a U-boat?"

"Yes. Like I said, Fort Meade kind of specialized in U-boats. There are several submariners buried in the cemetery."

Sawyer, who was only partly listening to the conversation, had his nose pressed to the glass of the display case and was carefully inspecting the black and white photos inside. He grinned at seeing the images of the sleek black hulls of the U-boats careening through the Atlantic waves. He turned to Tyler, touched his hand, and said brightly, "Look, Tyler, underseaboat."

Tyler felt the hair on the back of his neck rise. Did Sawyer speak German again, he asked himself? Was he struggling through the German word for submarine — Unterseeboot? Or was he just making up some childish word for submarines, like Griffin insisted?

Tyler leaned in over the child's shoulder and whispered to him, "Do you know those submarines? Have you seen them before?"

"I've seen them," Sawyer answered.

"Where did you see them?"

"They float in the ocean. They go under the water in the ocean and they have torpedoes."

"That's right," Tyler said, patting Sawyer gently on the back. "What else do you know? What can you tell me about the Unterseeboot?"

"Sometimes they sink and the people die. Sometimes they are bombed by planes and they blow up. No way out of them, so you just die."

"Sometimes you die inside, and sometimes you die in the water."

"Yes, and the water is very cold. I don't like cold water."

"Me neither," Tyler whispered, his mind suddenly flashing back on the day he had taken Sawyer to the lighthouse cistern and how just the smell of the cold, dark water inside had made him shudder. "I don't like cold water at all."

Tyler was holding his breath in anticipation. The museum had grown quiet and he realized Griffin and the old curator had paused in their conversation and were gawking at them. Griffin had the strangest look on his face — a mixture of great curiosity and restrained anxiety. Tyler swallowed hard and composed himself.

"If the submariners died here, where's the graveyard?" he asked.

CHAPTER SEVEN

Not being able to successfully follow the directions given to them by the museum curator, Griffin drove up and down the streets of Fort Meade until they came upon a large tract of land surrounded by a white picket fence. Nearby was an ornate wooden gate with a large sign reading CEMETERY. The boys parked on the grassy shoulder and wandered up to the gate only to find it secured with a heavy chain and padlock.

"That's tough luck, dude," Griffin said, turning to head back to the car. He hadn't taken even two steps however when Tyler vaulted over the fence. "What are you doing? Are you crazy?"

"I didn't come all this way just to be locked out," Tyler said casually.

"Dude, this's a military base. You can't be screwing around like this here."

"They're not gonna shoot me, right? It's a cemetery, Griff, not a missile silo."

"Yeah, well if you do get caught the first thing they're going to do is call Mom and then your whole great plan is going to be revealed!"

"Then I guess you better stop shouting at me before someone notices. Are you coming or not?"

Griffin marveled at how calm Tyler could be when breaking the rules. Granted, he had an impressive body of work in the area, but there was also a quality to the thirteen-year-old that allowed him to see his goals as being more important than other people's rules. This wasn't necessarily a bad quality, Griffin acknowledged. After all, history was filled with rabble-rousers who broke the rules and ended up changing the world for the better. He looked down at Sawyer who was staring back anxiously and it suddenly occurred to him that maybe this was exactly what Tyler was doing, in his own clumsy way.

"Okay, dude," he said to Sawyer, "we're going over the fence."

The boy nodded and with Griffin's help clumsily scaled the wooden slats. They joined Tyler and wandered down the narrow dirt paths between neat strips of tombstones separated by carefully manicured grass and scattered thickets of hickory and walnut trees. The cemetery reminded Griffin of others he had seen all over New England, especially those dating back to the 18th and 19th centuries. Judging from the tombstones, simple markers carved from light grey stone and encrusted with moss and lichen, no one had been buried here in a generation.

Tyler led the way, winding quickly through the headstones. As he wandered, he read the inscribed names aloud until Griffin eventually interrupted him and asked what they were looking for.

"German names," Tyler said.

"Big hairy deal, Tyler," Griffin moaned. "We know some of the P.O.W.s were probably buried here. The old guy at the museum told us that much. I'm not sure what you hope to prove by finding their graves."

"Sawyer," Tyler said to the little boy, "why don't you wait over by that tree. Griffin and me need to talk private, okay?"

Sawyer looked frightened and shook his head. "I don't like this place," he said. "Can we go back to the lighthouse now?"

"We will in just a little bit, okay? Promise. Just wait over there for a second. We'll be able to see each other so you won't get lost or anything."

"Are you guys telling secrets?"

"We're not telling secrets. It's just we need to have a private conversation for just a second."

"That's telling secrets."

"Just do it, okay? Promise we'll just be a second."

Sawyer didn't like the idea of moving away from the older boys. He had no way of knowing how many bodies lay hidden under his shoes or the stories behind the names carved on the monuments around him. He only knew the place smelled of rotting leaves and damp earth and the ground was spongy and squished softly every time he took a step. He knew this place was very old and he wondered if anyone even remembered to visit here anymore. He walked carefully to the hickory tree Tyler had pointed to, testing the ground with the toe of his shoe for fear he might fall through and find himself in an ancient tomb surrounded by dusty, cobweb-strewn skeletons.

Once Sawyer was out of earshot, Tyler whispered to Griffin, "I'm testing something, but you have to play along."

Griffin glanced over at Sawyer, who was now fearfully hugging the tree. "What are you testing exactly? How much you can traumatize that little guy? Dude, we shouldn't be bringing him to graveyards. Especially after how he reacted when you took him to the cistern. He has enough nightmares, doesn't he?"

"In all those books I read about reincarnation, there were a bunch of cases where people recognized their former life by seeing an old photo, or visiting their old house, or seeing their old grave."

"So that's it?" Griffin asked angrily. "You're gonna scare the crap out of him to see if he recognizes one of the German names on a tombstone here?"

"You heard him in the museum, Griffin. He was speaking German again. He was talking about being on a U-boat and how it felt to die in cold water."

"He says lots of things, Tyler. He's a kid. He never shuts up..."

Sawyer pressed his cheek to the scaly bark of the tree. It felt cold and moist. He kept his eyes glued to Tyler and Griffin, fearing that if he blinked they'd vanish and leave him stranded in this frightening place. He couldn't see Tyler's face, but he could tell by Griffin's that they were arguing. Around him, poking out of the ground like toadstools, were a dozen grave stones. He tried not to look at them. He figured if he didn't look, nothing bad could happen. He closed his eyes and hoped this would all be over soon.

"Besides," Griffin continued, "how on earth do you know we're in the right place? The museum dude told us that there were several places along the coast where German P.O.W.'s were taken."

Tyler sneered. "But this one specialized in men off of U-boats. I know this is the right place. Everything fits. If Sawyer was on a German submarine in a former life, then I know he's buried here."

"Do you know how crazy you sound?"

"Shut up, Griffin. Did we really come all this way not to try? You promised to help me on this."

"That promise didn't mean I was okay with turning that little boy's brain into mush. You're gonna freak him out doing this kind of stuff, Tyler. If he pees himself, I'm going to kill you."

At that instant, Sawyer began bawling, calling out to them between frantic gasps of air. Both boys leapfrogged over tombstones to his side. He was squeezing the tree with all his might, his eyes pinched shut and his teeth grinding against each other. Griffin wrapped his arms around him and patted him gently on the back.

"It's okay, Sawyer," he said softly. "We weren't leaving you or anything. What's the matter? What's freaking you out?"

"Pl-please," Sawyer choked, "I wa-wanna go home. I'm scared. I wanna go back to the lighthouse."

Tyler was oblivious to the child's cries, his eyes scrutinizing the entire area. What had caused Sawyer to freak out, he asked himself? There had to be some clue... something the kid saw.

"Tyler, we need to go now," Griffin said sternly.

"In a second," Tyler replied, waving him off.

Griffin was stunned. "God, dude, you're cold-hearted," he growled. Tyler wasn't listening however. He was bouncing from stone to stone, looking for some clue that he himself couldn't explain.

Griffin noticed a white SUV was passing on the street. The vehicle slowed and the men in military uniforms were staring at them.

This can't look good, Griffin thought. Two teenage boys in a graveyard with a bawling child. They probably think we're torturing him or something.

Images of Humvees stuffed with heavily-armed Military Police rolling up on the cemetery's perimeter filled his head. "Now, Tyler! Enough is enough!" he snapped.

Tyler's gaze skipped across the grave markers that surrounded them. Most of the tombstones were identical in their size and shape, but some were decorated with dried flowers or tiny American flags tattered by the sun and the weather. Then Tyler noticed a cluster of graves about ten feet to his left, decorated with small tri-colored flags of black, scarlet and gold. Odd names began to reveal themselves from the mute stone. Dates from the mid-1940s. Kreigsmarine, the German word for navy, popped out at him.

"This is it!" he cried, rushing over to the tombstones and scrapping the moss away with his fingernails. "Look! German names! These are the graves of the camp's prisoners of war! I told you Sawyer would find them!"

Griffin wasn't listening any more. What was I thinking, he admonished himself? I'm an intelligent person. I have a high school diploma and I'm attending junior college. Why am I creeping around in an old cemetery on the wacko theories of a thirteen-year-old?

He looked back at where the white SUV had been, but the vehicle had vanished. He picked up Sawyer and headed back to the car.

"We're leaving," he called over his shoulder to Tyler. "If you're not coming, I guess you better plan to live here."

Tyler dismissed Griffin's threat. He wasn't stupid. He knew Griffin wouldn't abandon him in Maryland, but he also risked upsetting him to the point where he'd refuse to ever help him again. But something compelled him to keep going, to use every second he had to search every stone he could. He knew this would be his one and only trip here. He had to make it count.

He moved faster, trying to pronounce the strange jumbled letters of the German names: "Ackermann. Keller. Neustadt. Schultheiss..."

He glanced over his shoulder but Griffin and Sawyer were already out of sight. A cold wind swept through the trees surrounding the graves. A handful of leaves fluttered in corkscrew paths to the ground. Tyler shivered and felt his back stiffen. He bit his lip and forced himself to focus. There wasn't time for him to lose it too.

Where had Sawyer been looking when he started to bawl, he asked himself? He continued to jump from gravestone to gravestone.

"Wagner... Lehmann... Gottschalk... Tschantz..."

That last name stuck in his throat for some reason. Tschantz. He squatted down by the marker, a somewhat eroded marble slab carved with neat letters and a simple cross above them. He dug the grime out of the capital "T" with his finger and flicked it onto the ground.

Ehren K. Tschantz
German Prisoner of War
Kreigsmarine
May 14, 1922 - January 17, 1945

He looked back at the hickory tree where Sawyer had been standing. It seemed possible the eight-year-old could've seen this headstone from where he was standing by the tree. The branches overhead suddenly shifted in the wind again and a ray of sunlight landed on the stone. A warm sensation pulsed through him, like the feeling you get when you swallow a mouthful of hot chocolate too fast. His lungs felt like they were burning.

In the distance, a car horn blared. Griffin was losing his patience. Tyler suddenly remembered the camera in his pocket. He pulled it out and snapped several photos before running back to the car and accepting that he had a long, unsatisfying road trip back home.

It was a somber winter morning. The sky over the fort had disintegrated into a mass of dark clouds which would occasionally dowse the iron gates, high walls and red brick buildings with a freezing rain. The snow on the ground had melted into a grey slush, which flooded the footpaths between the dormitories. Ehren

waited in the cold outside the main interrogation building with Lieutenant Spolarich.

"We're going to put you in the holding cell first," the lieutenant told him as his stamped his feet in a futile attempt to warm them. "I want you in the room before we bring in some P.O.W.s we took off a U-boat yesterday."

"Their boat was attacked?" Ehren asked.

Lt. Spolarich shook his head and chuckled. "Naw, they surrendered. Their boat was caught on the surface by some of our destroyers. Your comrades are running out of spare parts and fuel, so apparently they couldn't submerge. We got all the crewmen off but their captain scuttled the boat." He pulled a bundle of rolled papers out of his jacket pocket and handed them to Ehren. "These are the names of the men we rescued. Tell me if you see anyone who might know you."

Ehren scanned the list quickly. "It's hard to say," he replied, "but I don't think so. Most of the men I graduated and sailed with are dead or captured by now. This crew's probably new. I don't recognize any of these names."

Lt. Spolarich smiled and pocketed the papers. A guard cracked open a nearby door and told them the new P.O.W.s were headed over to the holding cells. Lt. Spolarich nodded and patted Ehren on the shoulder.

"Put 'P.O.W. Offerman' in the cell first so he's waiting for them," the lieutenant told the guard. "I'll have our men pull you out in a few hours."

"I understand," Ehren said, following the guard obediently.

He positioned himself against the far wall, underneath one of the swinging ceiling lamps where a microphone was hidden. After about ten minutes he heard the shuffle of dozens of feet and the clinking of chains on the corridor floor outside. He slouched against the wall and did his best to look bored and *irritated. The American guards opened the cell door and ushered a small group of submariners inside.*

My god, they all look so young, Ehren thought to himself.

In fact, the average age of the U-boat crewmen entering the cell was only nineteen years, although their spotty beards and shaggy hair made it difficult to see their youthful faces. The new arrivals looked guardedly at Ehren. Some exchanged an unenthusiastic "Guten tag!" with him, but otherwise were silent. After months of coaxing information out of his countrymen, Ehren had learned a lot about patience. Engaging in conversation too quickly usually aroused suspicion. It was always better to let the new P.O.W.s speak first.

After about an hour, the prisoners began to grow restless. Some climbed up on the benches to peer out the small barred windows which overlooked the camp's main compound. They chuckled about how ugly and cold America was, nothing like the golden land they'd heard about. Ehren found those comments bitterly ironic, considering their homeland was undoubtedly a pile of rubble.

"It's been like this for days," Ehren offered softly. "I don't think the sun will ever come out."

One of the men standing at the window glanced over at him. He was about twenty years old with dark brown hair and scraggly whiskers. He offered a sliver of a smile.

"How long have you been here, comrade?" he asked.

"Six days," Ehren answered. "It's been nothing but rain and snow the entire time. I haven't seen the sun yet."

The dark-haired man drew in a deep breath. "It'd be tolerable if you could at least smell the rain," he said. "Instead, all I smell are a bunch of stinking submariners!"

The men in the room began to laugh. Showers were virtually nonexistent on board a U-boat, so the crews became used to their own stink. From the look and smell of them, no one in the room had yet been offered a bath, a shave or a haircut.

Ehren smiled. "The Americans will let you bathe at least," he said. "If nothing else, there's plenty of hot water and soap here."

"Hot water and soap!" the dark-haired man cried happily. "I barely remember either!" He hopped down from his perch by the window and walked over to Ehren. "What's your name, comrade?"

Ehren saluted and replied, "Offermann. Heinrich Offerman."

"Pieter Ecker," the dark-haired man replied, returning the salute.

"I thought you might be submariners," Ehren grinned.

"Because we stink?" Ecker chuckled.

"No, because of your beards. When did the Americans capture you?"

"Two days ago. Our generator broke so we had to surface. No way to repair it so there we sat until two American warships showed up. Our glorious captain ordered us all to the life rafts and he and the commander sent the boat to the bottom of the Atlantic. At least we robbed the Americans of that!"

The other men let out a tired, somewhat futile-sounding cheer.

"Ecker," a large, angry-looking man snapped from nearby, "shut up!"

Ecker turned to look at him. "What is it now, Jungclaus? Can't we even talk among ourselves?"

The other man shifted. He was a great hulk, all shoulders and arms from what Ehren could see under his overcoat. "Now, that's just it," Jungclaus growled. "You don't know if your talk is staying among us, do you?"

Ecker snickered.

"Need I remind you," Jungclaus barked in a loud voice, silencing all the murmurs in the cell, "that you are sailors of the Kreigsmarine even in captivity. You're surrounded by the Fatherland's enemies and should assume that anything you say will be overheard by those enemies." He took a long look at Ehren, like a dog sniffing at a stranger through a garden gate. "As for this little mouse," he growled, "we don't know who he is so he's not to be trusted."

Ehren felt a chill run up his back, but experience let him hide it completely. Lt. Spolarich had prepared a convincing backstory for him, but there was never a guarantee someone wouldn't be able to penetrate his lies and expose him as a spy and a traitor. If that were to happen, it was doubtful the American guards could rescue him from the cell in time.

Ehren decided the best course of action was to agree with the giant man. "You are quite right, comrade," he said. "You don't know me and I don't know you. But can't I at least expect a little civility among comrades?"

Jungclaus snorted. "Civility? Where do you think you are, mouse? You're in an American prison. There's no civility in prison."

Ehren began to tell his tale, which was a combination of information supplied by the Americans and details which would only be known to a sailor in the German navy. He'd told the story before. He'd been questioned on the specifics enough that he had prepared answers and was so skillful in his delivery he made it sound completely credible.

Jungclaus seemed unconvinced but remained quiet. He turned his back to Ehren and limped to a bench on the other side of the cell.

"Are you injured?" Ehren asked.

"It's an old wound," Jungclaus replied. "Nothing I wish to share with you, mouse."

Ehren didn't attempt any more questions for another hour, instead sharing remembrances about his hometown and school days with several of the other submariners. From time to time, he'd notice Jungclaus glaring at him. Ehren tried to ignore the stares, to appear only as a bored prisoner of war. But there was something about the man that was very troubling. And there was something familiar too.

Eventually, however, Ehren remembered the hidden microphones overhead. He needed to produce something or the Americans might become irritated with him. He leaned close to Ecker and asked if there was any news about the war. He knew the microphone wouldn't be able to hear their whispers, but at least he could gather the information and the brute called Jungclaus wouldn't become more suspicious.

"We have very little news," Ecker told him quietly. "There are few dispatches from home and of course you never know what's true and what's propaganda. Our sense is that the war goes poorly for the Fatherland. Have you heard nothing here?"

"To hear the Americans speak, you'd think they'd already won," Ehren sneered. "But they don't allow any newspapers or radios, so you cannot tell for certain. Is the U-boat fleet still intact? Are our forces still able to fight?"

Ecker suddenly looked sad. "The wolf packs are only a shadow of what they used to be," he said. "Most of the men I knew on other boats I've never seen again. They go out on missions and never return. We don't know if they're captured or killed, we just know they never come back. The Atlantic seems to have more Allied ships than fish anymore..."

Suddenly Ehren felt himself being pulled off his feet and slammed into the concrete wall behind him. Above his head, the suspended light swung violently into the ceiling, its bulb popped in a flash of raw electricity and bits of broken glass fell into his hair and face.

Strong fingers clamped around Ehren's throat and pinched off his airway. In the darkness he could see Jungclaus's eyes staring into his.

"I said to be quiet, you treacherous mouse!" the man hissed, pushing on Ehren's skull with such force he thought it might crush his head completely.

The cell door swung open and Ehren heard a group of men yelling at the submariners in English. The hand on his throat fell away and he slumped onto the bench below. The American guards swarmed into the room, pounding on Jungclaus with truncheons until he collapsed onto the floor.

"Corporal, put them in chains and take them all back to the barracks! Heavy labor for the lot of them tomorrow!" one of the Americans yelled.

Ehren allowed himself a second to relax. He'd been wrong. The American guards could rescue him in time if he got in trouble.

"You!" one of the guards yelled at him. "Get up!"

Ehren was grabbed by the collar and yanked to his feet. Two of the guards began to place handcuffs and leg-irons on him. He looked around frantically for Lt. Spolarich or any familiar American face, but the cell was in chaos. More guards arrived and began hauling the Germans out into the hallway, delivering blows to their backs or legs if they resisted. Some of the submariners were fighting back which further increased the confusion in the cell. Ehren began to push back.

Don't they know who I am? Don't the guards recognize me? Where is Lt. Spolarich?

"Stop resisting us!" one of the guards bellowed at him, cuffing him on the side of the head with an open hand. He crumpled back onto the cell floor.

"Please! Please!" Ehren said urgently in German. "I did nothing! I'm supposed to stay in the cell!"

"Get on your feet!" the guard yelled again. Two more Americans half-dragged him to the cell's door where a sergeant was snapping out commands.

Ehren grabbed the man's arm and in English cried, "I'm not supposed to go with the others! Where's Lt. Spolarich?"

"Get off of me!" the sergeant yelled, belting Ehren across the chin with his free hand. Again he toppled backwards and onto the cell floor. He saw the one remaining light, with its secreted microphone, directly overhead. Was no one listening on the other end?

The guards hauled him back to his feet and put him in line with the other submariners for the march back to the barracks, a place where Ehren was never supposed to show his face.

Ecker was standing nearby. His lip was bleeding. He caught Ehren's gaze and said softly, "You speak English, comrade."

CHAPTER EIGHT

Ms. Trease was shelving books when Tyler suddenly materialized at the door of the school library. It had been nearly two weeks since she last saw him and she found herself missing their visits.

"Well, hi there stranger," she smiled. "Where've you been keeping yourself?"

Tyler shrugged. "I don't know," he said. "Just been doing stuff. Can I come in?"

"Of course you can," she said, setting the armload of books she was carrying on a nearby table. "Did you need help with your school work?"

He shook his head.

"Ahhh," she said with amusement, "you're still working on your personal project? The one about submarines?"

"U-boats, actually," he said.

"RIght, right. Well, how can I help you?"

Tyler walked over and laid his backpack on the table. This was the first time he'd approached Ms. Trease so directly and he felt completely self-conscious. He didn't trust adults by nature, but Ms. Trease seemed both kind and sincere in her desire to help him. Still, what he was about to share with her might change all that.

He unzipped the backpack and pulled out prints of the photos he had taken in the Ft. Meade cemetery. They'd become crumpled and some had peanut butter smeared on them. He quickly cleaned the photos on his pant leg and laid them before her.

"Now where were these taken?" Ms. Trease asked, pushing her glasses down onto the tip of her nose.

"My big brother drove me to this war museum in Maryland last weekend," he said cautiously. "They had a big display on U-boats and there was this graveyard where prisoners of war were buried."

"I see. And this is a grave of a German?"

"Yeah..." he said, but the rest of his thoughts stuck in his throat and he just stood there, open-mouthed, looking both expectant and ridiculous.

"Yeah? But?" Ms. Trease asked. She tilted her head slightly to one side and frowned at him. "There must be more to it than that?"

"I was – I was wondering if there's a way to find out more about this man, the one whose name's on the headstone?" he croaked.

Ms. Trease inspected the photos again. The nutty smell of them was making her hungry. She wondered if it was time to break out the afternoon snack she had routinely shared with Tyler during his visits. "The museum where you went didn't have any information on him?" she asked.

"My brother was anxious to leave so we didn't have time to ask."

"Well, let's jump on the internet and see what we can find. I subscribe to a website that let's you look up stories and names and places in different newspapers all over the world," she said, leading him over to her computer terminal. "Since we have this man's name and date of death, we could check the Maryland-area newspapers and see if there are any obituaries on him."

"Do you think that's possible?" Tyler asked.

"Pretty much every newspaper will have obituaries, but the big question is whether or not this man would appear in one since he was a prisoner of war. I don't know if they'd include him under those circumstances."

Tyler watched with great interest as Ms. Trease navigated through the newspaper archive, typing in Ehren Tschantz's name and date of death. A variety of hits were returned, but nothing seemed to match the exact person they were looking for.

She frowned. "What else can you tell me about this man? You took these photos in Maryland?"

"Yes, at a military base called Fort Meade."

"Wow. That's some amazing dedication on your part, Tyler."

"I know," Tyler replied, again feeling strangely self-conscious.

Ms. Trease entered the information and then filtered the results for a year both prior and after Tschantz's date of death.

"Now this's interesting," Ms. Trease whispered. "We're getting a lot of hits on a man with his name from several months after he died."

Tyler shivered. "Huh? That doesn't make any sense."

"I agree. Let's open some of these articles and see if this is even the same person."

Ms. Trease made a series of rapid clicks on her touchpad and the screen filled with a grainy black and white image of an old newspaper. The page was a hodgepodge of peculiar advertisements and photographs and tiny columns of text. She made a few more key strokes and adjustments and the image enlarged and refined itself. At the top of page was a bold caption which read DEATH OF P.O.W. AT FT. MEADE UNDER INVESTIGATION. Tyler tried to absorb the information, but his reading skills were poor and he quickly gave up. He'd let Ms. Trease distill it for him.

Ms. Trease whispered quietly to herself: "Interesting. Interesting..." She finally turned to Tyler and asked him, "How'd you come to have an interest in this particular P.O.W.?"

Now, how to answer that question, he wondered? Up to that point, Ms. Trease had been completely non-judgmental about his quest for knowledge, but then again she didn't know the full extent of his interest. Like most of the school's staff, Ms. Trease saw any interest of Tyler's outside of spitting on people or putting pieces of food up his nose as a pleasant change of pace. But after his trip to Ft. Meade with Griffin, he was feeling more circumspect about what he shared with others. If he told Ms. Trease his story, would it land him in more therapy sessions with Dr. Cardenas?

He decided to take a cautious approach and said blankly, "I'm just curious. I just saw the gravestone so I took a picture of it."

Ms. Trease stared at him for a long moment. Clearly she knew there was more to it than that, but she was too diplomatic to press the issue. She turned back to the computer and said, "The reason I'm asking is that this man, the one whose name is on the grave, was apparently murdered at this facility."

Tyler felt a great pressure in his chest, like an unseen hand had reached through his back and was crushing his lungs and heart.

"Tyler, are you okay?" she asked him.

"Huh?" he stammered.

"You just have a weird look on your face. Do you want some water or something?"

He shook his head. "Naw. I'm okay."

Ms. Trease bit her lip and said, "You didn't know this man was murdered?"

"No. Like I said, I just took a picture of the grave. How was he murdered?"

"This article doesn't really give many details," she replied. "It says that 'naval and army personnel found Ehren Tschantz, 23, a German prisoner of war, dead in his cot in a dormitory at Ft. Meade. Lieutenant James Spolarich, a spokesman for the Navy, refused to speculate on the cause of Tschantz's death pending an autopsy, but stated that foul play may have been involved.'"

Tyler pulled closer. The tightness in his chest was making it hard for him to breathe. Ms. Trease scanned through more pages.

"Here's another article," she said. "This is two months after Mr. Tschantz died. It says that although Naval officials concluded Tschantz had been murdered, they weren't able to identify a suspect in his death. Authorities thought he was probably killed due to his anti-Nazi sentiments. Do you want me to print these articles out for you?"

Tyler's mind was racing. He was astounded and baffled by how quickly new information was suddenly unfolding before him. For days, "Ehren Tschantz" had just been a name carved on a stone slab, but with a few finger-strokes on a computer keyboard he suddenly had a story and a history and a drama all his own. Tyler found himself agonizing over how this German's personal tragedy blended with that of the eight-year-old who slept across the hall from him every night. But there was a new sensation as well, one Tyler hadn't felt before. It was as though he had opened a mystery book which had been collecting dust since 1945 and found the last few pages to be blank. Suddenly, everything was pointing toward a conspiracy.

What worried him most however, was not how this story would end but whether it would ever be believed by another human being. Tyler didn't suffer from an excess of credibility anyway, and believing an eight-year-old child was somehow connected, through some mysterious mechanism of time and fate, to a long-dead German sailor was not likely to help his reputation.

For a second, he even wondered if he was just losing his mind.

"Tyler?" Ms. Trease said again, touching him gently on the hand.

The touch startled him, but he was able to refocus quickly. He looked at her and said somewhat obtusely, "Print what?"

"These articles, dear. Would you like me to print these out for you?"

"Sure, sure. I mean, yes, please."

He spent another hour with Ms. Trease pouring over the internet database but unfortunately wasn't able to find many more details about Tschantz's death. The U.S. military had been particularly secretive during the war years and additional articles only stated that several other German P.O.W.s had been detained for questioning but authorities didn't have enough information to charge anyone in the killing.

As Ms. Trease sorted and stapled the various pages, she watched Tyler from across the room. For the first time in the two years she'd known him, he seemed utterly lost in his own thoughts. Quiet and pensive, he was suddenly a far cry from the impulsive, often out-of-control boy she usually encountered. But Ms. Trease saw a lot more on Tyler's face than deep concentration. He seemed genuinely disturbed by the information they'd just uncovered.

She tapped the short stack of papers into a neat pile and handed them to him. Tyler immediately wadded them up and stuffed them into his backpack. They too would smell of peanut butter by the time he got home.

"I don't suppose you'd tell me what this's all about?" Ms. Trease asked.

Tyler shook his head. "I'm just curious is all."

"You're sure? There's nothing else I can help you with?"

He slung the backpack over his shoulder and started walking quickly for the door. "I'm sure," he said.

And then, if only to underscore Ms. Trease's suspicions that there was something truly different about him, he thanked her for her help before running off into the late afternoon sun.

The march back to the P.O.W. barracks was the most terrifying experience of Ehren's life since he had swum furiously through the frigid Atlantic waters and away from his burning submarine. His mind raced as he thought of ways to escape this situation. He didn't dare speak English again. The submariner called Ecker had already overheard his words to the American sergeant, had already heard him ask for an American officer by name. He had to think quickly of an excuse, to buy himself some time until Lt. Spolarich realized the mistake and pulled him out of the P.O.W. barracks.

He began to hold his head and moan softly in pain. The Americans and the Germans ignored him.

The prisoners' barracks was a long, narrow room lined with metal cots and little else. It was big enough to accommodate about ten men, but was sparse when it came to amenities. As the American guards paused to remove their shackles, Ehren made a quick head count. There were eight others in the barracks. He didn't like those odds.

Despite the cramped conditions, Ehren recognized the German sense of military order in that the hall was spotlessly clean and well-organized. There was a wooden footlocker with each cot and short piles of neatly folded blankets arranged on top. There were no showers, only a semi-private lavatory with a short stack of porcelain wash basins and clean towels sitting on a table. Two tall thin windows covered with bars filled with room with a hazy grey light and Ehren could clearly hear the raindrops beating against the glass panes.

Although it had a lot of the same furnishings as his private quarters, he suddenly missed the little comforts Lieutenant Spolarich had provided over the last few months, including the crackling radio where he could listen to news and music every night; or the colorful pages he'd neatly torn out of the Saturday Evening Post to decorate the walls with images of the rocky but beautiful New England coast.

The American guards pushed them all inside and slammed the metal door behind them.

"Please," Ehren called through the door's window to the guard. In his desperation he chose to use English again. It was his only hope of getting out of the barracks. "My head is injured. I need to see the medical officer."

The Americans did not reply.

The men in the barracks began to cluster into groups, talking about what had happened in the holding cell. Nearby, Pieter Ecker was gazing curiously at Ehren.

"You speak English?" he asked.

Ehren nodded. "Just enough to get by," he responded. "My mother spoke it fluently."

"If you're injured, you should sit down," Ecker said, gesturing to the cot nearby. "I doubt if the guards will listen to you, even if you do speak English."

Ehren limped over to the cot next to him. He sat with his back against the wall so he could watch the rest of the room. At the other end of the hall, Jungclaus and several other men whispered angrily among themselves.

"Is it your head?" Ecker asked.

"Yes." Ehren rubbed his brow and grimaced in pain which was only partly pantomimed. "Thanks to your comrade who thinks he's the camp commandant. He slammed me against that wall so hard I could have a concussion."

"Some men lead by example, others by force," Ecker murmured. "Imagine what is was like being onboard ship with him?"

"What happened to his leg?" Ehren asked. "Why does he limp?"

"He took a bullet there almost a year ago when our boat was attacked by American bombers. There wasn't a doctor on board so it didn't heal correctly. So now he limps."

"You were attacked? When was this?"

"Last May. We were refueling when the planes spotted us. The men on the other boat hadn't freed us from the refueling lines, so he ran out of deck and chopped us free with an ax. Jungclaus is an ass, but he saved us all that day."

A hard, painful lump had appeared in Ehren's throat. "What happened to the other boat?"

"Gone. Destroyed." Ecker frowned. "Are you all right, comrade? You look terrible. Shall I call the guard and tell him about your head? I don't know if it will help. They won't understand me."

Ehren glanced at the metal door again. "When will they come back?" he asked.

Ecker shrugged. "There's no way to tell. But rest here if you like. Eventually we can let them know you need to see the physician."

"Thank you, comrade."

For the next hour it was quiet, although the small congregation that had formed at the far end of the barracks had now grown to include every man in the room except Ehren and Ecker. And other than Ecker, none of the submariners from the cell had attempted to re-engage Ehren in conversation, which in itself was very unsettling. He fought to control his emotions. Ever since the men had come in the middle of the night and hauled his father away years earlier, Ehren had found reason to be afraid of other Germans. Some families had experienced far worse, however. Two months after his *father had returned from prison, a Jewish family living down the street was arrested and bundled off in broad daylight. The secret police didn't even bother to be secretive. That family never returned. Their home was soon turned over to non-Jewish Germans who were also Nazi Party members. No one ever asked what happened to the original occupants or questioned how their entire house and all their property suddenly belonged to someone else. Yes, fear of other Germans was something Ehren understood well. He tried to chat with Ecker, but he was suddenly paranoid about everything he said. In the cell with the hidden microphones he'd always felt in control. Here he felt lost.*

At about 9:00 p.m., several American guards came through the barracks and Ehren was successful in engaging one of them in conversation. Making his English sound as broken and unpracticed as possible, he told him that he needed to see a doctor for his head. He didn't dare ask for Lt. Spolarich again. Ecker hadn't asked about his earlier slip of the tongue and Ehren was hoping it'd been forgotten.

The American guard looked Ehren over suspiciously. "The doctor's left for the night, Fritz," he snickered. "You'll have to wait until morning."

"Please," Ehren whispered. "This is an emergency. I must see the doctor at once."

The guard guffawed. "Do you think I was born yesterday, Fritz? Now shut your cake-hole. You'll wait until morning."

The lights snapped off and the barracks fell into a sinister silence. The rain clouds had lifted, at least for the moment, and moonlight flooded in through the barred windows and painted the walls with a strange variegated pattern. It was barely enough light to make out the configuration of the room, but not enough to see any further than ten feet away. Ehren pulled a blanket over him and peered into the darkness. He listened for any sign of movement from the far end of the room where

*the other submariners were resting. Everything was
quiet. He vowed not to sleep a wink. He would remain
vigilant until dawn. He'd survive this like he survived
everything else.*

*Despite his best efforts, Ehren had fallen asleep
and had dreamt of his father. He had seen him as a
grizzled and skeletal figure chained to a wall in a damp
cell. He didn't know what his father's experience in the
Nazi prison camps had been like, as the old man had
never spoken of it after his release. But Ehren imagined
it to be like something out of the French gothic novels
his mother had read to him as a boy, with great stone
catacombs lit by flickering torches, floors littered with
the bones of past victims and echoing with the moans of
hundreds of dying men. He dreamt of the Nazi prison
guards dressed in black hoods and medieval armor. He
dreamt that the air was heavy and hot and burned as you
tried to breath. He dreamt that he was gasping for
breath.*

*He opened his eyes but everything was blurred.
He tried to scream but a large calloused hand was
clamped over his mouth. He heard whispers around him.
Whispers in German.*

*As his eyes adjusted to the dim light, he saw
Jungclaus towering over him. Several other men were
clustered around the cot and were holding down the
edges of his blanket so he was unable to move his arms
or legs.*

*"He's the one," a voice said. "He was waiting in
the cell before anyone else... All alone and asking lots of
questions."*

*Another said, "No one knows who he is. He
didn't arrive with anyone here. He must be an
American!"*

"No, he's obviously a German. He knows too much about the naval service. He was a sailor somewhere."

"When he was in the cell downstairs, he was speaking English to the American guards," said another voice. It sounded like Ecker. "I don't know what he was saying, but he seemed to be asking for someone by name."

"Then he's a traitor, working for the Americans," said another voice loudly.

"Be quiet. The guards will hear," Jungclaus snapped. He moved his face closer to Ehren's and whispered, "Tell me who you are, mouse. Are you a spy?"

Ehren could scarcely breathe, let alone speak, beneath Jungclaus's powerful grip. He could have said many things, but doubted any excuse would have satisfied this man. Defiantly, he squeaked, "I'm one of the few survivors of the U-boat you killed."

Jungclaus looked perplexed. At first, he didn't understand what Ehren had said. But then there was a flash of realization Ehren could see wash over the man's face even in the darkened room. Did Jungclaus remember him, he wondered? Did he remember the man standing on the stern of the other U-boat all those months ago, pleading with him not to cut the fuel lines that tied the two vessels together? Until this moment, Jungclaus had never thought of that man or imagined what his fate had been; and whether it was bad luck or providence which brought them together again didn't matter. Ehren's suspicions had been correct. Nothing he could've said would save him.

"What did he say?" one of the other men asked. "We didn't hear him."

"He's confessed," Jungclaus replied. "Hold him still."

The hands on him tightened. Jungclaus pulled the pillow out from underneath Ehren's head and pushed it down over his face. Ehren could not scream, could not breath, could not think. His lungs gasped for air, but there was none. The pressure seemed to crushed his heart and lungs. He suddenly couldn't hear the voices anymore or feel the hands which held him to the mattress.

And then everything just stopped and Ehren Tschantz ceased to be.

CHAPTER NINE

Lane and Tracy, the young couple who had come with the Cowgirl and brought Sawyer arm-loads of brightly-wrapped presents, had returned every weekend since to usher him away on various outings. They'd even taken the boy back to Freddy Fuffenagle's Pizza Emporium and this made Tyler feel angry for some reason he couldn't quite understand. Sawyer had come home from the trip and presented Tyler with a large handful of candy, fake spiders and wax lips. The gesture only made him feel worse and it became harder and harder for him to summon any happiness for Sawyer's good fortune.

Lane and Tracy's increasing number of visits had succeeded in distracting Sawyer from any further investigation about U-boats, German submariners and creepy old graveyards. The boy was now much more interested in spinning long tales about Lane and Tracy's big back yard filled with beautiful trees dripping with aromatic fruit; their twin Golden Retrievers named "Anakin" and "Padame;" and how his new room had a large fish-tank filled with tiny red-finned sharks and a plastic treasure chest which popped open every few seconds in a cloud of bubbles.

Even more maddening was the fact that Lane and Tracy showed up for each visit in clothes that were completely free of wrinkles.

At first, Tyler didn't know why their wrinkle-free outfits upset him so much and he spent hours wondering how they managed to keep themselves looking that way when they were carting around a rowdy and very messy eight-year-old. Frankly, it seemed unnatural. He briefly entertained thoughts that they were vampires, or extraterrestrials in human form, or some kind of evil clones whose excessive neatness betrayed their inhuman nature. He didn't let himself believe his resentment came from being jealous, although he certainly was jealous. Instead, he had decided that how Lane and Tracy dressed showed a certain level of arrogance. What were they thinking, he asked himself as he looked at his own rumpled appearance in the bathroom mirror? Do they think their nice home, new car and bundles of presents will solve all of Sawyer's problems? Wrinkle-free clothing and fish tanks with bubble-blowing treasure chests don't mean anything. They're just distractions but Sawyer will still be Sawyer and his past and his phobias will still be there. Lane and Tracy will learn that the first time the boy throws himself onto the floor in a crowded restaurant and screams curse words they never heard before because he didn't get a refill on his Dr. Pepper. So much for the perfect little angel they see during their visits.

Tyler grinned at the thought of this and tried to smooth down his messy hair with his hands.

Eventually Sawyer's day trips with Lane and Tracy developed into overnight visits where he was allowed to stay in his new bedroom. Tyler had become used to the little boy snoring softly on the other side of the hallway and he found himself missing him more and more. He was hiding behind the boxwood shrubs one evening when the couple's shiny sedan came rolling up the driveway after a long weekend visit. Everyone was laughing as they climbed out of the car and Sawyer immediately grabbed onto Tracy's outstretched hand. Tyler clicked off his flashlight and sat quietly. He noticed Lane and Tracy had bought Sawyer some new luggage for his visits — a large duffel bag decorated with Bugs Bunny in a baseball outfit with the words "Way To Go Slugger!" emblazoned across the sides.

As they walked up the path to the front porch, Sawyer pulled Tracy over to the boxwoods and squatted down in front of them.

"Tyler, are you in there?" he called.

Tyler hesitated. He wanted to be cruel. He felt if he ignored Sawyer it would punish him for his happiness. After a second though, he replied with a simple, "Yeah."

"Mommy and Daddy got me some new video games," Sawyer squealed. "Do you wanna play them? We can take turns."

"Uhhh..." he hesitated again.

Tracy bent low and peered between the thick branches and tiny clusters of leaves. "Tyler, why are you sitting in there?" she asked.

"That's his secret place," Sawyer answered. "It's cool back there. It's a hideout."

"I think it's probably very dirty and yucky," Tracy answered. "Does Karen know you go back there?"

"Probably," Tyler said. "She doesn't care."

"She doesn't care that you come into her pretty house all covered in dead leaves with your clothes all dirty and wrinkled?"

Tyler thought: See! There's the obsession with being wrinkle-free! Lady, you gotta be some kind of evil clone. But he replied: "No, she doesn't care."

"Well, I think she probably cares."

"Tyler, do you wanna play my games with me?" Sawyer asked again.

"Not right now," Tyler said. "Maybe later."

"Mommy," Sawyer asked, tugging on Tracy's hand, "when I move into your house can Tyler come over and play with me?"

There was a hesitation in Tracy's reply which lasted only a second or two, but to Tyler it betrayed her thoughts before she even verbalized them. "Well, sweetie, we'll need to check with Karen about that. I'm sure we can discuss it."

Tyler knew this was a cop out and he wondered if Sawyer did too. Anytime adults said "we can discuss it" or "let me think about it," they were really saying "no" but trying to avoid an argument. Tyler sat still, holding his breath. He wanted Sawyer to challenge the lady in the wrinkle-free clothes, to speak up, to rebel just a little. But instead the boy nodded obediently and said nothing.

"Let's go inside and you can play your games," Tracy suggested, leading him away. As they climbed the steps to the front door, she turned to Lane and said, "Do you know that Tyler's hiding in those plants?"

Lane shrugged and replied, "That's his hideout, honey."

Tyler remained behind the boxwoods for several minutes listening to the disturbingly unwrinkled adults chatter with Karen about their visit with Sawyer, then he crawled out and snuck away into the darkness. He didn't want to be there when Lane and Tracy came back out. He didn't need another lecture. He didn't need to feel guilty just because he wanted some time alone.

He wandered around the side of the house and over to the edge of the yard where he could hear the surf lashing against the rocks below. A crescent moon sat on the horizon and its milky light sparkled against the ocean's surface. He turned and looked up at the lighthouse's tower. Through the narrow windows he could see the strands of decorative lights hanging from Griffin's ceiling and hear the muffled guitar riffs from his stereo. He really want to just sit and talk with Griffin like they'd done for years, but things had been tense between them since the visit to the Fort Meade graveyard. Although Sawyer hadn't mentioned a thing about the trip — and frankly didn't seem to care about it one way or the other — Tyler felt Griffin had been quietly blaming him for somehow traumatizing the boy. Since then, he and Griffin only spoke a few words at a time and usually only in passing.

From inside the house there came a series of electronic pings and boings followed by Sawyer's shrieks of delight and Lane's booming laughter. The boy had found someone else to play video games with him. Tyler's mood darkened.

Carefully avoiding the adults and Sawyer, he crept into the house through the back door, tiptoed up the crooked staircase and tapped on Griffin's door. The teenager cracked the door open and peeked out at him.

"What's up, dude?" he asked.

"Do you want to hang out or something?" Tyler asked.

"Sawyer's home. Don't you want to do something with him?"

Tyler shook his head. Griffin frowned and then motioned him into the room. They stood quietly looking at each other.

"Are you mad at Sawyer because he's not spending so much time with you anymore?" Griffin asked.

Tyler snorted sarcastically. "No. I don't care about that." He looked sheepishly at Griffin and asked, "Are you mad at me?"

"A little," Griffin confessed. "But I'll get over it. I don't like how you've been acting, man. You're being really creepy about this whole reincarnation thing."

"Huh?"

"Seriously, dude. I mean, it was a fun little adventure for a while but you seem absolutely obsessed with it now."

Tyler felt betrayed for the second time that evening. He could feel his face becoming hot. "I thought you believed it too?" he said.

"I find it interesting. I don't know how much of it I really, truly believe. How could you really believe it because there's no way you can really prove it?"

"I can prove it," Tyler said defiantly.

"How?"

"When we find the men who killed Ehren Tschantz, Sawyer will recognize them. He'll be able to tell the police what they did, how they committed murder. They'll get in trouble for it."

"Wait a second. What're you talking about? What murder?"

"I know the name of the man Sawyer was during World War II. His name was Ehren Tschantz and he was murdered at that base we visited. Ms. Trease, our school librarian, helped me find some newspaper stories on it. The navy did an investigation but they never found the murderers so Ehren Tschantz was buried in that graveyard and forgotten."

"Dude, how would you come up with a name like that?"

"I figured it out. When Sawyer was freaking out in the cemetery, he was standing near the grave of Ehren Tschantz. That's how I knew. That's how it works. He saw something from his former life — he saw his name — and then he started to remember. That's why he freaked out."

Griffin was silent for a second as he collected his thoughts. "Now that's what I mean when I say you're becoming obsessed about this."

"Shut up, Griff. I'm not obsessed."

"Maybe Sawyer freaked out 'cause we stupidly took him to a graveyard? Most eight-year-olds don't dig on that kind of thing, Tyler."

Tyler shook his head. "He's remembering it. He's remembering his past life. I know it."

"Okay," Griffin sighed, "for grins let's say you're right. Let's say that Sawyer is the reincarnated spirit of — what's his name?"

"Ehren Tschantz."

"Ehren Shanks?"

"Tschantz."

"Tschantz?"

"Right. Tschantz."

"Okay, Tschantz. It's a sixty-year-old murder, Tyler. If the navy couldn't figure out who did it at the time, what makes you think you can figure it out after all these years? If the murderers are still alive, they're in their eighties or nineties and they probably live in Germany."

"Maybe not. We have a secret weapon because we have Sawyer and inside him is all the knowledge and memories of Ehren Tschantz. We just need to pull them out and we don't have much time because soon Lane and Tracy are going to take him away and then we'll have lost our only chance to find the truth."

Griffin took a deep breath and put his hand on Tyler's shoulder. The gesture surprised and confused him and for an awkward moment he thought he was going to get hugged again. After all, Griffin wasn't really a touchy-feely guy. If he made physical contact with you at all, it was usually during the administration of a purple-nurple.

"Dude," Griffin said softly, "do you really think Sawyer cares about the truth?"

Tyler was shocked. "What? Of course he cares."

"Really? He's eight, Tyler. He's interested in television and playing with his Legos. He's getting new parents and a new home. With all that good stuff going on, why would he care about World War II or submarines or a murder that happened so long ago no one even knows about it but you?"

"He's been coming along and helping us. Why would he do that if he didn't care?"

Griffin shrugged. "Maybe because he likes being with you, he thinks you're cool. But my question is... why do you care?"

Tyler gulped. His head hurt. Why he cared wasn't a question he'd ever asked himself. "People shouldn't get away with it when they do bad stuff," he said.

"Tyler, who is it you want to punish here? It is a bunch of old Germans who may or may not have killed someone decades ago? Or is it about you wanting to punish someone who hurt Sawyer? I know how protective you are of him, but you can't punish the people who have hurt him. It's a nice thought, but it's not something a thirteen-year-old can do."

"You're talking like my therapist," Tyler sneered. "I hate it when people tell me what I'm thinking or feeling. You don't know."

"Naw," Griffin said, "I don't know. It's just my opinion."

He took his hand off Tyler's shoulder and retreated to the other side of the room. There was a hard silence between them.

"Are you mad at me again?" Tyler asked.

"I'm not mad at you, Tyler," Griffin smiled gently. "But you need to think about what you're doing and why. There are some battles you just can't win."

Lt. Spolarich was stirring his morning coffee with the end of a pencil when a knock came at his office door. A military policemen stood in the doorway and saluted stiffly.

"Sir, you're needed in the prisoner barracks immediately," the young man said uncomfortably. "There's a problem."

It was not even 6:00 a.m. yet, the lieutenant mused, what could possibly be the problem? The base was just beginning to awaken and the Germans wouldn't have even been assembling in the mess hall for breakfast yet.

"What is it?" Lt. Spolarich asked, distractedly moving some of the stacked files on his desktop from one corner to the other.

"One of the P.O.W.s was found dead in his bed, sir," the guard replied.

It had rained all night and was expected to continue through the afternoon. Lt. Spolarich, in his haste to follow the MP, had forgotten his coat and his hat and was deeply regretting it by the time they'd crossed the quad and entered the dormitories. Now he was cold and his uniform speckled with rain, which was not the way he wished to present himself before enemy prisoners. There was always a certain posture one needed to show to P.O.W.s. Showing weakness or vulnerability — even through something as simple as a forgotten overcoat — could invite dissent or worse. As a result, the lieutenant felt inadequate and strangely fearful as he wound his way through the unusually large contingent of guards assembled inside the upper hall.

Sadly, prisoner deaths weren't an unusual occurrence at the base. Many German P.O.W.s died from injuries or sickness shortly after they arrived, often conditions they'd sustained during their capture. But having one expire in the dorm itself was peculiar. If the dead German had been so medically fragile that he died during the night, why hadn't he been sent to the infirmary? But once Lt. Spolarich made it through the doorway into the long chamber lined with cots, it became immediately obvious this was no ordinary death. The Army sentries had moved all the Germans to the far end of the room near the lavatory and had them sitting cross-legged on the floor. The room itself appeared to be relatively normal. The P.O.W.s had risen at dawn when revelry had sounded and had promptly dressed, made up their cots and stowed their gear in typical military fashion. Everything was neat and precise, except for the one body still lying in a bed to the lieutenant's right. The man was completely covered with a blanket, with only a few wisps of dark hair showing at the top.

A sergeant approached Lt. Spolarich and saluted. He stood close to Spolarich's shoulder and spoke softly so the prisoners wouldn't overhear. "Sir, when my men came in today to escort the P.O.W.s to the canteen, they noticed that one man had not left his bed. At first they thought he was sick or had overslept, but he didn't respond to verbal commands so they attempted to rouse him physically. Again he didn't respond. It was then they noticed the man was cold and stiff and had obviously been deceased for many hours."

Lt. Spolarich moved closer to the cot where the body was strewn. Even though covered in a wool blanket, the position of the corpse was unnatural. The arms were placed along the sides of the body and his legs were pointed straight out. Most people didn't sleep so neatly. It was almost as though he had been arranged in that position.

"None of the P.O.W.s said anything to the guards about him?" Lt. Spolarich whispered to the sergeant.

"Not a word, sir. In fact, according to my men, they pretty much ignored the body altogether. You should take a closer look, sir."

Lt. Spolarich knelt down next to the man's right arm. He reached below the blanket and touched the wrist and found it icy. He carefully pulled back the blanket and realized the dead man was still fully dressed in his the cotton shirt, blue denim trousers and work boots issued to all P.O.W.s. The man's mouth of agape and his eyes partially open. Blue eyes.

It hadn't occurred to Lt. Spolarich, even as he knelt there looking into Ehren Tschantz's lifeless face, that this could possibly be his prized stool-pigeon. Tschantz's presence in the dorm was so out-of-context for the American officer that it took a moment for his brain *to process who he was seeing. The U.S. military had elaborate precautions in place to make sure enemy soldiers who turned against their countrymen were protected. It wasn't lost on anyone how much these men jeopardized themselves by cooperating with the Allies; nor how much the Allies relied by these rare individuals to betray everything they'd been taught to believe and serve. Lt. Spolarich couldn't understand what had gone so wrong that Ehren Tschantz would be in this room in the first place. The fear smouldering in his chest was immediately replaced by rage.*

The sergeant squatted down on the other side of the cot from Lt. Spolarich and muttered, "He's one of your fellas, isn't he sir?"

"Yes." The lieutenant felt himself flush. "What the hell was he doing in here?"

"Yesterday afternoon there was a fight in the holding cells," the sergeant replied. "The P.O.W.s were removed back to the barracks and put on lock-down. In the confusion, the guards brought him back here with the others. Once the mistake was noticed, the officer-on-duty decided to wait until morning to pull him out because it'd be less obvious to the other prisoners than yanking him out in the middle of the night. It was a quiet night, sir. The guards reported no sounds of a struggle or anything that indicated a problem."

"I guess I don't have to point out to you the error with that observation, Sergeant?" Lt. Spolarich seethed.

"No, sir."

Lt. Spolarich struggled to collect himself. He needed to look poised and strong when he stood up from the cot. He could feel every pair of German eyes watching him from the far end of the hall. Before he rose, however, he gently closed Ehren's eyes with his thumbs. He asked, "How'd they kill him?"

117

The sergeant shrugged. "Not sure, sir. There aren't any wounds or marks on the body that we could find. My guess is they probably smothered him."

"Do any of the prisoners have injuries?"

"Sir?"

Lt. Spolarich motioned stiffly to Ehren's body. "This man was no 90-pound weakling, Sergeant. He had to put up a struggle."

"I've not seen any obvious bruises or injuries on the other prisoners."

"I want to look around," Lt. Spolarich announced, walking quickly to the far end of the room. As he passed through the cluster of Germans sitting on the floor, only one lifted his eyes to meet him. A large man with huge arms and massive shoulders. The lavatory was immaculate. The wash basins were all clean, dry and neatly arranged on a table top. The rest of the hall was perfectly in order. If it hadn't been for the corpse lying in the cot, it would've seemed like any other morning.

The sergeant frowned at him. "What would you like me to do, sir?" he asked.

"Inspect all the prisoners, Sergeant. Strip them down to their all-togethers and see if you find any scratches, bruises, anything like that. My guess is they used blankets to restrain the man they killed, like putting him into a straight-jacket. That's probably why your men didn't hear a struggle. They overpowered him as he slept and then kept him immobile while they killed him."

"How do you want to handle interrogating them, sir? We have eight suspects in here."

"Separate them all and keep them separate. Every single one of them knows what happened and who did what. We'll have to wear them down to get to the truth."

CHAPTER TEN

What had become clear in the four days since Ehren Tschantz's death is that the murderers had found a very effective way to hide in plain sight. They'd spent the hours after the murder deciding what they were going to say (or not say) once the body was discovered. Without exception, all eight men claimed they were asleep when the attack on Tschantz had occurred. As a result, the Americans still couldn't determine if this group contained one killer or eight. The Germans' denial of responsibility had been so consistent that one of the American guards had wondered aloud if someone unknown had crept into the barracks, killed Tschantz and then crept back out again without any of the P.O.W.s noticing. Lt. Spolarich kicked him out of the room for suggesting something so absurd.

Still, for the lieutenant there was a sense of tragic absurdity about the whole event. It was absurd that a man as valuable and vulnerable as Tschantz had been placed in the barracks to begin with, an act which was like putting a lamb among wolves and then expecting the creature to make it through the night untouched. There was an absurdity to the logic of the night duty officer who discovered the mistake but made no effort to contact Lt. Spolarich and took no action to rescue Tschantz for fear of blowing his cover. There was the absurdity that the German P.O.W.s felt for an investigation into the death of someone who was clearly a traitor during a time of war. After all, they complained among themselves, would American P.O.W.s in German camps have acted any differently if they knew a stool pigeon was among them? And finally, Lt. Spolarich felt as though he was personally absurd, first for befriending Tschantz when he should've kept him at arm's length, then for failing him with such terrible consequences.

The fact that Lt. Spolarich grieved for the twenty-three-year old submariner was something he kept to himself. Already some of the higher-ranking officers were asking pointed questions about the "excessive privileges" Tschantz had received, including the use of a radio and a rumored nighttime trip to the local movie theater. Lt. Spolarich knew it wouldn't benefit him to appear to be soft on any German in the fort, especially if the Army and Navy were looking for someone to blame for the death since wringing confessions out of the P.O.W.s had been unsuccessful. In what he hoped would finally bring about some positive results, Lt. Spolarich arranged for a lie-detector to be used on the German prisoners. The strange device was a conglomeration of knobs and flashing lights which charted the subject's heart rate and other vital reactions on a rolling drum of paper. If the prisoner lied, so Lt. Spolarich was told, there would be an automatic physical reaction which was beyond human control. The lie-detector's operator could determine what answers were false by watching how the machine's needles moved. It was desperation which prompted the lieutenant to call for the device, but quietly he wondered how effective it could possibly be. After all, if exposing a lie was as easy as watching the movement of an electric gauge, why wasn't every criminal in the country caught and successfully prosecuted?

The answer to that question lay in the details. It was clear after the first day of operating the machine that every German in the barrack the night Tschantz was killed knew about the murder. What the lie-detector couldn't tell Lt. Spolarich is who'd done what. The technology, as impressive as it was, still hadn't revealed a clear suspect in the killing and left Lt. Spolarich with the poor choice of either prosecuting eight men with no proof or confession or letting all of them go free. The days of slogging through questions had produced two men who were at least more emotional about the circumstances of the crime than the others. One was a U-boat engineer named Pieter Ecker and the other a hulking Petty Officer named Hans Jungclaus. The latter man was particularly vocal about the need for traitors to die. Lt. Spolarich had decided to concentrate his interrogation efforts on Jungclaus.

The door to the room opened and two guards led in the massive submariner. Lt. Spolarich dismissed his melancholy thoughts for the moment. He couldn't afford to be distracted. The technicians began to wrap Jungclaus in wires connected to the lie detector, which proved difficult due to his girth. The man didn't resist or question the process. He glanced up at Lt. Spolarich, his brown eyes narrowing beneath eyebrows so blond they almost appeared white. It was a look of both defiance and supreme confidence.

The machine was switched on and began to hum. The technician fiddled with some knobs and then turned to the lieutenant and announced they were ready to begin. The technician spoke to Jungclaus in his native German, beginning with a series of control questions used to establish the man's normal heart beat and respiration level. Even before the first question was asked, it was clear to Lt. Spolarich how confident Jungclaus was of his ability to beat his interrogators. He was what the naval intelligence officers referred to as a *"true believer," a man so dedicated to the Nazi cause that he'd gladly give up his life to protect it.*

The polygraph test was difficult to complete due to the German's unwillingness to confine himself to simple "yes" or "no" answers. Instead, like a true believer, he wanted to lecture and moralize. This irritated the polygraph technician, but for Lt. Spolarich it was extremely revealing. He knew from experience that men who liked to talk usually ended up saying too much. During the interviews, the Americans used Tschantz's cover name so as not to reveal the truth about his activities at the base.

"Was Mechanikerobergefreiter Heinrich Offermann murdered on the night of January 17th?" the technician asked.

"I don't know what happened to him," Jungclaus replied. "I was asleep in my cot."

"Confine your answers to only 'yes' or 'no,'" the technician instructed him. He repeated the question.

"No, I don't believe he was murdered."

"Was Mechanikerobergefreiter Offermann executed on the night of January 17th?"

"I don't know."

"Again, confine your answers to 'yes' or 'no.'. Do you know who killed Mechanikerobergefreiter Offermann?"

"No."

The technician glanced quickly at Lt. Spolarich. That was a lie, obviously.

"Did you have any discussions with other German prisoners about Mechanikerobergefreiter Offermann?"

"That wasn't his name," Jungclaus growled, leaning back in his chair and crossing his arms over his mammoth chest.

"Would you please confine your answers —"

Lt. Spolarich interrupted the technician and asked, "What do you mean when you say that wasn't his name?"

Jungclaus grinned mischievously. "Whoever that man was, 'Heinrich Offermann' wasn't his name."

"Why would you say that?" Spolarich asked. "You didn't know him, did you?"

"No one knew him. In fact, the only time anyone ever saw 'Heinrich Offermann' was in those holding cells, asking lots of questions. Under those circumstances, I assume 'Heinrich Offermann' was a fictitious name."

"Do you know everyone in the German Navy by name? If you never met the man, how could you just think his name was fictitious?"

"It was," Jungclaus said confidently. "I know it was."

"And based on your assumption about his name, you decided he was a spy?"

"I never said he was a spy, although that'd be a logical assumption for a man with a fictitious name."

"And if he was a spy, you and your comrades in that dormitory would've tried to execute him for this crime?"

"As I said, I know nothing about the circumstances of his death. I was asleep when this event happened. But..." Lt. Spolarich held his breath, hoping for the confession he'd been trying for days to extract, but the German was too intelligent and would deny him that prize. "If he was a spy, then it would've been necessary for him to die."

"And if he wasn't a spy, then you and your comrades committed cold-blooded murder," Lt. Spolarich replied.

"I didn't murder anyone. I know nothing about a murder. I'm simply saying, hypothetically, that if he was a spy the rules of war would've required him to die."

From a military point of view, Lt. Spolarich knew that made sense. Only two years earlier, eight German spies had been deposited by a U-boat on the New England shore with orders to blend into the American public and carry out various sabotage missions against power plants and factories. All eight were quickly captured and six of them were executed by the U.S. military using the same logic the hulking German was describing. But Lt. Spolarich had a harder time putting Ehren Tschantz into the same category as Nazi saboteurs. Maybe because Tschantz shared Spolarich's belief that the only way the world would survive the twentieth century was to eliminate fascism completely. Maybe because Tschantz suffered as much as anyone under the Nazi regime. Maybe because Tschantz was a simple, kind man who liked American Big Band music and dreamed of a day when he could sit on the banks of the River Seine and paint the sun rising over Paris.

"And you and the other men in that room decided to carry out his death sentence?" Lt. Spolarich pressed.

Jungclaus chuckled mockingly. "You're not going to get me to confess to a murder," he said. "I know nothing about a murder. But whatever Fate had in store for your man, 'Offermann,' was obviously in the best interest of Germany and the Fuhrer."

There was a long silence between the men, each waiting to see what the other would say next. The polygraph technician was leaning his chin against one hand, exasperated by the interrogation. The results of the test were useless but Lt. Spolarich didn't care. He knew he was looking into the face of the chief conspirator and probably the man most responsible for Ehren Tschantz's death. He knew this young German, wrapped in wires and surrounded by his enemies, would never give up himself or any other man in the dormitory on the night in question. Although a captive, he was still at war and would never surrender.

Lt. Spolarich leaned in across the table, staring Jungclaus directly in the eyes. "I know you killed him," he said. "And if it takes me until the end of time, I'll bring you to justice."

Jungclaus smiled again. That confident, infuriating smile. "American," he said, "you don't have until the end of time."

CHAPTER ELEVEN

It was only a few weeks until Halloween and Ms. Trease was changing the library display case to feature materials with a decidedly spooky nature. She'd pulled a large stack of the books from the regular collection including titles on sea monsters, psychic phenomenon, ghosts and haunted houses; as well as works of fiction about boy wizards, teenage vampires and journeys to mystical lands. But the title she placed in the center of the window and then strung with fake cobwebs and plastic spiders, was about reincarnation. She'd done so quite unknowingly, subtly inspired by all those conversations she'd had with Tyler about past times and forgotten lives.

Neither the principal nor any of the teaching staff could quite figure out how she'd managed to build such a good rapport with a kid who nearly everyone else just hoped to avoid. Ms. Trease wasn't able to explain her success either. Maybe it was just as simple as being interested in what he had to say? Even without Tyler present, Ms. Trease found herself staying late after school to cruise the internet for more information about U-boats, the Second World War and the death of the German sailor named Ehren Tschantz.

Teenagers slowly began to fill the hallway, yelling at their friends or banging their locker doors. Tyler's arrival was announced by the shouts from a girl he was chasing with a spit-covered finger. Ms. Trease couldn't help but smile a little. In a way, she felt sorry for the kid. He was always true to himself, but it was that quality so many others found repulsive.

"Get away from me, you freak!" the girl yelled at Tyler, making a few angry swipes at him with her pre-algebra book.

The students around him were already rolling their eyes or walking in the other direction.

"Tyler!" Ms. Trease called to him over the din.

He looked up, alarmed and half-expecting to see a teacher armed with a referral slip or the assistant principal who always had one chair reserved in his office just for Tyler. Instead, he was met with Ms. Trease's smile. The young girl he was tormenting took advantage of the distraction and quickly ducked into the crowd, delivering one parting thought — "You're disgusting!" — before she vanished into the sea of bobbing heads and shuffling feet.

"I was just teasing," Tyler told Ms. Trease sheepishly.

She shrugged. "I'm not worried about that. Come inside for a moment. I have something for you."

She led him to her desk and handed him a neatly stacked and stapled pile of papers. They were copies of old newspaper articles.

"I hope you don't mind," she said, "but you piqued my interest about this man, Ehren Tschantz, so I did some more digging on him."

Tyler thumbed the edges of the papers. He asked himself: she doesn't actually think I'm going to read all this, does she?

Ms. Trease saw his hesitation and decided to summarize the packet for him. "After that German sailor was killed, there was a trial," she started.

"A trial? Of the person who killed him?" he asked.

"No, actually the Navy never seemed to figure out who the murderer was. The trial was of a Naval officer, the man who was supposed to be protecting Tschantz. His name was James Spolarich. Remember, he was quoted in some of the old newspaper articles right after the murder happened?"

Spolarich. What a strange name, Tyler thought. "Why'd he get in trouble if he didn't have anything to do with the murder?" he asked.

"That's a good question. Maybe you'd like to ask Mr. Spolarich himself?"

Tyler glanced around quickly. "Is he here?" he exclaimed.

Ms. Trease giggled. "No, but after I found out about his trial, I did a search on his name and found a man listed as 'Captain James B. Spolarich, U.S. Navy retired,' who lives about an hour outside of town. I think it must be the same person. There can't be too many men with that name who also served in the Navy."

"Yeah, it's a weird name."

"If you want... after school... come back by and we can call him. I found his home telephone number and maybe you can ask him a few questions about Ehren Tschantz?"

That hot stone which always sat in Tyler's chest whenever he was feeling anxious materialized again.

"Is that okay?" Ms. Trease frowned.

"Huh?"

"You have a strange look on your face. You don't have to do this unless you want to."

"Naw... I mean, no... I'm okay." He paused and then asked, "Do you really think someone's still around who knows about this?"

"Well, Captain Spolarich's would be a very old man now but he could still remember these events. I guess the only way to know for sure is to ask him. I'll help you if you like?"

"Okay," he replied hesitantly. "I would like that."

Despite how his morning began, Tyler's school day didn't degenerate into the usual pattern of saliva-related hijinks followed by after-school detention. He was too distracted, staring off into space or doodling on his desktop. Several times his caught himself thumbing through the packet of papers Ms. Trease had given him; or trying to spell the name 'Spolarich' on this desktop before rubbing out the letters with his thumb. Most of his teachers took this change in routine as a welcome break and left him alone to daydream.

After the final bell had rung, Tyler loitered on the baseball diamond before walking back to the library. For whatever reason, he didn't want anyone to see him with Ms. Trease or overhear any conversation they might have with this old man, Spolarich. When he finally presented himself in Ms. Trease's doorway, the librarian was stringing a row of ghost-shaped light bulbs around the edge of the check-out counter.

"There you are!" she cried. "I was beginning to think you'd forgotten."

"No. I was just delayed."

"Well, come on in. I don't know if you're hungry, but I have some hummus and carrot sticks if you want a snack. It's very nutritious."

Tyler wandered over to her desk. "What's hummus?" he asked.

"It's kind of like a bean dip. You can eat it with bread or vegetables or whatever you like. Have some." She pushed a small plastic tub toward him with her pinkie finger. Inside was a substance which looked like pale yellow spackling paste topped with spices and chopped nuts. Tyler gingerly dipped a carrot stick into the mixture and rolled it onto his tongue. It was cold and tangy and not the least bit what he'd expected. The librarian's generous gesture amused him. He recognized Ms. Trease was trying to bond with him through the sharing of strange foods. Leave it to a teacher to bring something healthy when a box of donuts or a bowl of bite-sized candy bars would've worked much better, he thought. He ate a few more mouthfuls while Ms. Trease rummaged for Capt. Spolarich's telephone number.

"Did you think about any questions you might like to ask?" she called.

In fact, Tyler had no idea whatsoever to say to Spolarich. As the day had progressed, he'd felt that hot stone in his chest grow larger and more uncomfortable. He'd even entertained the idea of just leaving on the afternoon bus and telling Ms. Trease he'd forgotten about their appointment. He probably could've put her off for days until she finally gave up on him. The only thing which prevented him from doing so was his timid respect for the woman. But honestly, Tyler was terrified. So he decided to pass the buck.

"Will you talk to him first?" he asked. "He might hang up on me. He might think I'm pulling a prank on him or something."

Ms. Trease smiled gently and answered, "Okay. I'll get things going and we'll see if he's even receptive to the conversation."

She sat down across from Tyler and slowly punched Captain Spolarich's number into her cell phone. It seemed like they waited forever until the ringing on the other end ceased and a man's voice said briskly: "Good afternoon!"

"Hello? May I speak to Jim Spolarich, please?"

Tyler strained to hear the man's voice, but the sound was not much louder than the buzzing of a bee. He didn't sound angry or annoyed. Not yet, at least.

"This is Jim."

"Sir, you don't know me," Ms. Trease said, "but I'm a middle school librarian and I'm helping one of my students with a research project. To make a long story short, we found some old newspaper articles online about the death of a German prisoner-of-war that occurred at Fort Meade in 1945. Those articles mentioned a Lieutenant Jim Spolarich as being in charge of that investigation. Sir, would you happen to be that Jim Spolarich?"

She paused for a long time as the buzzing in the ear-piece continued. Tyler was studying her face carefully and he tried to assess the the tone of the call. Her brows lifted, then fell and creased. She bit her lip, then smiled a little. She said "yes" and "I see" about half a dozen times. Then she looked at Tyler and silently mouthed the words: "This is him!"

"Yes, sir," she said, smiling. "That's exactly the case we're interested in. My student's name is Tyler and he's looking into this story as a matter of personal interest. Would it be okay if I put him on the phone with you so he could ask some questions? That wouldn't be an intrusion would it? Oh, that's wonderful. Thank you so much for this... "

She held the phone out to Tyler and he gingerly placed it to his ear. He opened his mouth to speak, but his words jammed in his throat as he was suddenly swept with a wave of fear unlike he'd ever known before. He looked at Ms. Trease panic-stricken, resisting an urge to just snap the phone shut and run off.

"Go ahead," Ms. Trease whispered gently. "He sounds very nice."

Tyler took a deep breath and said meekly, "Hello?"

"Hello there, young man," the voice on the phone said. The man sounded kind, even jovial. "My name's Captain Spolarich and I understand you have some questions for me?"

"Y-yes," Tyler stuttered. "I'm... uh... I mean..."

"Don't be nervous, young man. I can't bite you through the phone, can I?"

Tyler grinned. "I just wanted to know... I wanted to know if you knew him?"

"If I knew who, son?"

"Did you know Ehren Tschantz?"

"Yes, I did know him. I knew him very well. Can I ask you why you're interested in Ehren?"

"I got interested in U-boats and stuff 'cause of my little brother. He's interested in them you see, so I started reading about them. Then I found out about Fort Meade and Ehren Tschantz. I didn't think anyone would still be alive who knew him."

Tyler cringed as soon as those words slipped from his lips. Dang it, he thought, did that sound rude? But his concern was unnecessary as Captain Spolarich was laughing. "Well, to tell you the truth, no one's asked me about Ehren in many, many years. And you're probably right that there aren't many people left who knew him or knew what happened to him. So what would you like to know?"

Tyler's head was swimming. What did he want to know? He had so many questions about the murder and why Captain Spolarich stood trial afterward, but he was so self-conscious all he could muster was to ask: "What was he like?"

There was a puzzled silence on the other end of the phone. "Oh my," the Captain responded finally, "that's not the question I was expecting you to ask."

"I'm sorry. Did I say something wrong?"

"Heavens to Betsy! No, you didn't say anything wrong. What was he like? Well, he was an intelligent man and one of strong conscience."

"What did he like to do?"

"I'm not sure what you mean, son?"

"What was his personality like? What did he like to do?"

"Goodness, you really are interested in Ehren. This's for a class assignment?"

"Um, kind of. It's for extra credit. But like I said, it's really because of my little brother."

"Your little brother's interested in Ehren Tschantz's personality?"

"Um, no. I guess I'm interested in that."

There was another long pause. Tyler waited anxiously for the line to go dead, but instead Captain Spolarich seemed to be organizing his thoughts. "Well, you definitely have some unique questions for me, son," he said. "I could probably spend an hour telling you all about Ehren, but can I ask you a question first?"

"Okay. Sure."

"How old are you?"

"Thirteen."

"Just thirteen... and interested in a man who died decades before you were even a twinkle in your daddy's eye. That's most unusual, Tyler."

"I have some really different interests from other kids," Tyler said, somewhat defensively.

"No doubt about that!" Captain Spolarich answered. "Well, I tell you what... Why don't you hang onto my telephone number and maybe you and I can get together and I will tell you all about Ehren face-to-face. You need to talk it over with your mom and dad, though."

"I don't have a mom or dad. I have a foster mom."

The Captain paused again. "Okay then, talk to your foster mom or have her give me a jingle. I could meet you at a restaurant or something and then we can have a nice long chat. I have some photos and things you might like to see, too. How does that sound?"

"Okay," Tyler said. "I will ask her and then call you back."

"I'll look forward to hearing from you," the Captain said. "Goodbye."

When the line went dead Tyler handed the cell phone back to Ms. Trease who was staring at him expectantly.

"So, he wants to meet you?" she asked.

Tyler nodded. "Yes, but he said I need to arrange that with my foster mom."

"Absolutely right," she said. "I'll even call your mom and tell her about this, okay?"

"Okay."

"Tyler?"

"Yeah?"

"Was the phone call helpful to you?"

Tyler stopped to think for a moment. He suddenly noticed the hot rock sitting in his chest was gone. "Yes," he replied. "It was very helpful."

It was raining again on the morning when an old lorry pulled into the grass on the side of the road and three men in green fatigues hoisted a coffin off the tailgate and began to carry it toward the trees. Lt. Spolarich and the base chaplain had been waiting nearly forty-five minutes for the lorry to arrive, sitting in awkward silence in the former's car. The chaplain had been smoking one cigarette after another in an attempt to warm himself, but all he'd managed to do was fill the car's interior with enough foul-smelling fumes that Lt. Spolarich found it difficult to breathe. Despite the offensive-smelling smoke, the lieutenant had chosen to remain quiet and polite. As a gesture of respect for the murdered man, the chaplain had decided to wear his ecclesiastical robes and perform a graveside service. It may be the only official acknowledgement of Ehren Tschantz's sacrifice, the lieutenant told himself. He'd suffer the fumes and the lingering stench it would leave in his car and his uniform for that scrap of respect.

"Perhaps we should go ahead and walk down?" Lt. Spolarich suggested, cracking open the car door and letting a billow of smoke escape into the cold winter air.

The chaplain, who was only half way through the current cigarette, glanced around and replied, "No one else is here yet."

"Honestly, Chaplain, I don't think anyone else is going to show up."

The chaplain pursed his lips and reluctantly tossed the cigarette onto the roadside. He bundled up his robes with one arm and stepped awkwardly onto the wet grass. "I didn't think it would be this soggy," he moaned. "It's going to be a muddy mess graveside, isn't it?"

The lieutenant nodded. "Yes, sir. It may be. You might want to hold up your robes."

The short walk down the path was a tiring process with the chaplain struggling to manage his cumbersome outfit while avoiding mud puddles and struggling not to slip on the slick grass. Lt. Spolarich had only been to the cemetery twice before, both times to bury German prisoners who'd died from their war wounds. But those times had been profoundly different. He hadn't grown to know those men like he had Ehren. It hadn't bothered him that no one but the necessary workmen and religious representatives from the base had materialized at those burials as well. It seemed to him, however, that this particular German deserved something more.

By the time they made it to the grave's edge, the men from the lorry had already lowered the casket. Its wood surface was dappled with rain drops and smeared with muddy fingerprints. The chaplain's remarks were brief. Lt. Spolarich suspected he'd shortened the service in consideration of the cold, wet conditions. When he was done, Lt. Spolarich signaled to the men nearby who removed a canvas tarp from a large mound of dirt and began to fill in the grave.

"If it's okay with you, Lieutenant," the chaplain said, his teeth chattering slightly, "I'm going back to the car and have myself a smoke."

"Of course," Lt. Spolarich smiled, shaking his hand. "I'll be up as soon as they've finished here."

The chaplain nodded and turned to leave. "Oh, you have a visitor, Lieutenant," he said.

Major Sharpe was lumbering down the path.

"Good morning, sir," Lieutenant Spolarich said, saluting.

"You call this a good morning, Jim?" the major grumbled. "Lousy weather. Lousy cold. A lousy morning to give any man his burial."

"Yes, sir. I must admit I'm looking forward to the springtime and a little more sunshine."

"I see the chaplain was all decked out for this."

"Yes, sir. I don't know how he'll get the mud out of those robes."

"Mmm... Well, it was a nice gesture."

They stood quietly, shoulder to shoulder for a moment, watching the soldiers nearby fling great clods of earth into the grave.

"You heard that the Army shipped out your suspects the other day?" Major Sharpe asked finally.

"Yes, sir. They're sending them to Arizona I believe."

"That's the plan."

"So the investigation's officially closed then, sir?"

"It is. Which is why I wanted to come down here and talk to you. I figured this's as about a private a place as you'll find on base. Jim, I know the last week has been hard on you and we both know you're getting a raw deal on this whole ugly incident..."

Lt. Spolarich felt his shoulders seize. It was an involuntary reaction and it reminded him of how angry he really was. "Thank you, sir," he answered. "I appreciate you saying that."

"Jim, I need you to let sleeping dogs lie. I know how stubborn you are and how much this poor boy's death has insulted your sense of right and wrong, but you're looking down the business end of a court martial on this and pressing an investigation which is no longer your concern isn't going to help."

"With respect, sir, we have a murderer — maybe several of them — who has yet to be identified and punished."

"Yup... and it's probably going to stay that way." Major Sharpe lowered his voice and said in a husky whisper, "Right now, Jim, the brass is asking more questions about the liberties you gave the dead man than about who killed him."

"That's ridiculous."

"Of course it is, but they don't have a whole lot of sympathy for any German, and certainly not a German turncoat. You and I both know that Tschantz probably saved countless American lives with the information he provided, but our command staff still see him as a traitor to his own people. They don't have any respect for him."

"I know. Strangely, sir, I think he knew that too. He thought his purpose was more important than his future."

The major shrugged. "And perhaps it was. But his future's gone and yours is in question. I want you to know that I'm going to do everything in my power to take some of the heat off you, but you've got to help me here. Stop asking questions because they're not going to get you anywhere. Unless one of the men in that dorm room suddenly has a crisis of conscience, we're never going to know for sure who killed Tschantz. Not in a hundred years."

The soldiers had finished filling the grave and asked for permission to leave. Lieutenant Spolarich waved them on and they slogged back up the path and disappeared.

"I have to tell you honestly, sir," the lieutenant said, "I'm having a really hard time letting this go."

"You need to find a way," the major replied. "Tschantz's gone and nothing you do is going to change those circumstances. Face it, Jim, sometimes the bad guys win."

CHAPTER TWELVE

True to her word, Ms. Trease had called Karen and informed her of Tyler's research on U-boats and his conversation with Captain Spolarich. As with so many of the things Tyler did, this too was met with a sense of surprise and some trepidation. Surprise because Karen was receiving a phone call from a school official and it wasn't bad news. Trepidation because try as she might, she couldn't understand Tyler's interest in these people and events when all his previous sources of amusement had involved throwing things, breaking things or putting things up his nose. Karen was careful not to criticize his new fascination, but she also kept waiting for the other shoe to drop. She felt guilty in suspecting Tyler was up to something, and probably to rebuke herself for her suspicions, she agreed to let him meet Captain Spolarich as long as he did so in a public place and in her company. Tyler, who was feeling increasingly private about the meeting, asked if Griffin could go with him instead. Griffin had agreed, feeling more charitable toward Tyler since they'd cleared the air between them. Plus, as much as he tried not to admit it, Griffin was curious about Ehren Tschantz and astounded by how many resources Tyler had mustered in his search for answers.

The meeting was set for a Saturday afternoon at a local all-you-can-eat buffet restaurant. Captain Spolarich told Tyler he should look for a man in a bright yellow World War II veterans cap. How much time had passed since Ehren Tschantz's death had not really impacted him until he saw the bright yellow cap being worn by a man in his late-eighties leaning on a rosewood cane. The Captain's hands were curled with arthritis and he was clearly blind in his left eye as the pupil was pearly white and didn't move. He was dressed oddly in an oversized flannel shirt, a large hooded coat, baggy trousers and red canvas sneakers. For whatever reason, Tyler had expected a much younger man in a military uniform.

Perhaps he can't see to dress himself, Tyler wondered?

The Captain seemed to recognize who Tyler and Griffin were, perhaps being the only elderly person in the place holding a meeting with two teenage boys, and waved at them with twisted fingers.

They spent a few moments on introductions and then the Captain suggested they hit the buffet before beginning their conversation. With plates piled with fried chicken and mashed potatoes, they found a secluded booth in the back of the restaurant and the old man began his long story about Ehren Tschantz. There was a certain hesitancy to how he spoke, as though he was choosing which details he would share. Still, Tyler and Griffin received a detailed sketch of Tschantz's life, from his rescue off his sinking U-boat, to his recruitment as an American spy, to his subsequent murder at the hands of his countrymen. It was the murder that prompted the greatest number of questions.

"Why didn't you arrest anyone?" Griffin asked, after listening open-mouthed to the Captain for nearly forty-five minutes.

"Who would we have arrested?" Capt. Spolarich answered, a decades-old wave of frustration sweeping through him. "There were eight men in that room and every blessed one of them knew about that murder. But when we asked them, when we put them under hot lamps and yelled at them for hours to get them to confess, not one of them turned over. Probably because they knew if they did, what happened to Ehren would happen to them too. You have to understand that there weren't just Germans in that room. There were some die-hard Nazis in there too, men who believed heart and soul in what Hitler was doing and would sacrifice their lives to protect his twisted dream. Or kill someone who got in its way. Ehren wasn't a true believer. He wasn't a Nazi. He was a poor kid who was born in the wrong place at the wrong time. He did what he thought was right to defeat the Nazis and end the war and... in the end... it got him killed."

The Captain was pensive for a moment. His right hand shook just slightly as he reached for his fork and awkwardly lifted a dollop of mashed potatoes to his mouth. He chewed slowly and as he set the fork down it clattered against his plate. After a moment, he asked, "Tyler, when you called me you wanted to know who Ehren was, what he was all about. Do you know what he dreamed of becoming and how he wanted to spend his life?

Tyler shook his head.

"He wanted to be a painter," he said. The word 'painter' cracked in his throat as it was coming out. The Captain's defective eye grew wet and a milky tear appeared at its corner. "He wanted to move to Paris and study at one of the art academies. He was even learning French in school. But then Hitler came and there wasn't much use for artists or novelists or thinkers in Germany. If you didn't have some practical skill that would benefit the war effort, well, good luck making a living. So Ehren gave up his dreams of being an artist and went to work in a shop that repaired lamps and radios and other electric devices. He became interested in radio and that was a skill valuable aboard a U-boat. He hated it. But he did what he had to to get by, to survive."

It suddenly occurred to Tyler that the old man wasn't speaking about a foreign prisoner of war, but about someone he liked.

"He was your friend," Tyler said.

Capt. Spolarich turned and looked at him. One eye saw the thirteen-year-old boy sitting across from him. The other one, the blind one, was still seeing a face from a very distant time and place.

"Yes, he was my friend," the old soldier said, "or as much as two men under those conditions in the middle of that particular war could be friends. I respected what Ehren was trying to do. A lot of the fellas I served with, well they" — he chuckled but it was an uncomfortable sound — "didn't have much respect for him, let's just put it that way."

Griffin furrowed his brow. "I don't get that. Tschantz was helping our side, helping us to defeat the Nazis. Why wouldn't any American respect him for that? He had to be taking a terrible risk."

"Hell's bells!" the Captain cried with a roll of ironic laughter. "Had he survived the war, he would've never been able to return to Germany. And I guess that's why I respected him, because he was willing to give up everything to do what he knew was right. He could've just sat out the war quietly in some P.O.W. camp but he wanted, maybe even needed, to do something to make sure the Nazis didn't win."

The three of them sat silently for a moment, then Captain Spolarich reached into his oversized coat and pulled out a bundle of old photographs bound with a rubber band.

"Now, I remember saying I would bring you some photos right?" He began to lay the snapshots out on the table top. Most of them were tiny, black-and-white images which smelled of musty paper. Tyler immediately recognized several of the buildings at Fort

Meade. Other photos were clearly of Captain Spolarich, although he was wearing the single silver bar of a lieutenant and was dressed in a light-colored uniform with a peaked cap. Tyler thought he looked kind and trustworthy. He also felt a vague sense of pity for the man. It was hard to imagine the young, vital officer in the photographs was the same broken down wreck sitting across the table from him. The passage of time since Tschantz's murder was suddenly so visible to Tyler's eyes. He could see it in every line in the Captain's face.

"Where are the pictures of Ehren Tschantz?" Tyler asked.

Captain Spolarich looked surprised. "I'm sorry, son, I didn't think about bringing any with me. That was a stupid oversight, I guess. I can get you some if you're interested."

Tyler nodded, disappointed but careful not to show it. Showing a photo of the dead man to Sawyer might provide that final bit of recognition. "So what happened to the other men?" he asked.

"Hmm?"

"The murderers. What happened to them?"

The Captain took a long breath and replied, "I served in the Navy, you see. The P.O.W. camps, however, they were run by the Army. Once those men were interrogated about Ehren's death, they were put on trains and shipped off to various camps all over the United States. After they left Fort Meade it was hard for me to track them and most I never heard about again. Plus, at the time, I had my own problems."

"What do you mean?"

"I was responsible for Ehren, you see. I thought of him as a friend, but he was also someone I was supposed to keep safe. When he ended up dead, smothered by a pillow in his own bed, it was me the Navy blamed. They wanted to try and hang the Nazis who had committed the crime, but since we were never able to get a confession, those P.O.W.s got away with it. Instead, I was the one who went on trial. Court-martialed for failing to protect my prisoner."

"I read some old newspaper articles about that," Tyler said. "That's kind of how I found you."

The Captain chuckled again. "Yeah, I was a bit of a news-maker at the time. The court-martial found me innocent of any wrong-doing, but it didn't matter because the accusation was enough to ruin me. I was in the Navy for almost another twenty years after that. I went to Korea during that war and was in a combat zone for two years. But I never made it higher than a captain. Ehren's murder followed me around until the day I retired."

"So you don't know what happened to the Germans?" Tyler asked again.

The Captain shook his head sadly. "No. After they left Fort Meade I never saw any of them again. I assume they returned to Germany after the war ended, which was just a few months after Ehren's death."

"Do you know where we might start looking for them?"

The Captain looked at him from the corner of his eye and began to quickly bundle the old photographs. "I'm sorry," he said gently. "It was a very long time ago and I'm sure most of them are dead by now. If others are still alive, they're old fossils like me. I can't help you with that, Tyler."

"Okay," Tyler said. It was clear the lunch was now over, but Tyler wasn't quite sure why. Had he said something wrong? What else was new?

After the Captain replaced the photos in his coat, he smiled weakly and said, "I'll find those photos of Ehren for you, though. Why don't you call me in a couple of days and we'll plan to meet again?"

Sawyer left Karen's lighthouse for the last time on a Friday afternoon. He was so excited about moving in with his new parents he neglected to say a proper good-bye to anyone other than Karen. He didn't think of his departure from the lighthouse as a permanent thing. He imagined coming back there again to hang out in Griffin's room, swinging in the hammock while he played video games. Or maybe he'd crawl beneath the boxwood shrubs with Tyler to share a bag of barbecue potato chips. It was unlikely, however, that any of that would happen. Tracy and Lane had a different vision of how they wanted Sawyer's childhood to progress and Tyler knew it didn't include him. He knew Tracy and Lane just considered him a strange, surly boy who pushed his way into other people's conversations and whose poor reputation extended well beyond the lighthouse's walls. And then there was that early incident in the bathroom where he had flooded the house. And that one where he took Sawyer to play around an old cistern and nearly fell in in the process. When the Cowgirl had told Tracy and Lane about that, it had pretty much sealed their impression about Tyler. Perhaps they thought he was reckless... or maybe just nuts. Whatever their reasoning, Tyler knew they didn't want him to be a part of Sawyer's future.

He stood obediently on the front porch next to Griffin and waved to the departing car with no enthusiasm or sincerity. He just felt numb inside. Once the vehicle had disappeared from sight, the Cowgirl turned to Karen and smiled.

"This is going to be such a good fit for him," she beamed. "I really want to thank you all for your help with Sawyer. I know he really felt comfortable and appreciated here."

Karen nodded. "He's a great little boy. I think they'll be very happy."

The Cowgirl picked up her briefcase and sighed. "Well, I have to finish some paperwork back at the office and then I'm heading home for the weekend. Karen, I'll call you on Monday because I may have some new placements for you."

"Sure. Just let me know."

Tyler grimaced at the thought of new foster kids. Would they wet the bed or steal from him or tell lies to get him in trouble? Would they be gone in a month or two like Sawyer, leaving Tyler behind again as the lighthouse's only semi-permanent fixture?

"I'm going to my room," he grumbled.

"Okay," Karen replied. "You were a very good friend to Sawyer, you know."

Tyler nodded stiffly. "Whatever. He's just a little kid."

"Well, it's important for little kids to have older kids they can look up to. You were really his hero, Tyler."

He didn't reply, letting the screen door bang behind him as he entered the house and ran up the stairs. He paused for a moment in the doorway of Sawyer's room. Karen had already stripped the sheets off the bed and a mop and bucket were standing at attention nearby. She'd have the entire room scoured down by the end of the day and ready for another child to occupy it. What number had Sawyer been? The tenth? The eleventh? He couldn't remember anymore.

He wandered down to his own room and stood for a few minutes at the window, staring across at the huge blue expanse of the Atlantic Ocean. The sky was clear and the sea was calm. A cool breeze blew in through the window and ruffled Tyler's tangled mass of hair. He sat down on the edge of his bed and felt a sharp jab in his right hip. He reached around behind him and pulled a Lego construction from the rumpled covers. It was a submarine, obviously placed there by Sawyer before he'd left. But the childish gift didn't make Tyler feel any better. If anything, it just reinforced his sense of isolation. He was like the old lighthouse which surrounded him: lonely and obsolete.

His despair turned to rage.

For the next half an hour, Tyler destroyed his bedroom. He smashed his belongings and tore his books to shreds; he flung his clothes out of his closet and across the room; he hurled anything he could lift until the floor was covered with chunks of plaster and the walls were covered with craters. Karen and Griffin had stood at the doorway trying every verbal trick they knew to calm him, but nothing worked. In the end, only the arrival of two police officers ended the destruction. He was calm as they handcuffed him and led him to the squad car. In a way, he felt better. Rage was something he knew and understood well, and the relief from having expressed it wasn't diminished by the fact he'd be spending the night in juvenile detention.

"What's wrong with you?" one of the police officers asked him. Tyler rolled his eyes. Like most adults in a position of authority, police officers had a lecture prepared for every occasion and would deliver it with little or no invitation. "You live in an amazing house. Man, if I had had an entire lighthouse to run around in when I was a kid, that would've been a paradise. I don't understand why anyone would treat such a wonderful place with such disrespect?"

Well, if you don't understand then I won't try to explain it to you, Tyler thought. Now here's where you tell me how cruelly I was treating Karen and Griffin...

"I mean, your foster mom and foster brother obviously work really, really hard to make a nice home for you," the officer continued, "and this's how you repay them? That's nuts, man. Don't you think that's nuts?"

Tyler ignored him, turning to look out the window as the trees and streetlights flew by. He wasn't going to make his situation worse by arguing with a cop about his motivations for doing this or that. Heck, he didn't even talk about that stuff with Dr. Cardenas. He did know, however, that it had nothing to do with Karen or Griffin. He wasn't attacking them or trying to destroy their home. The thought of hurting them had never even entered his head... and truthfully he couldn't remember what he was thinking as he flung objects around his room. He just knew it would make him feel better, if only for a short time.

He spent the next five hours in a small detention cell lying on a narrow cot and staring up at the ceiling. A single light hung above him, the bulb flickering and crackling. He found himself wondering if the detention officers had hidden a camera in the light. If they did, he thought, they're going to have hours of very boring footage to review.

In the very early morning hours he was returned to Karen and both of them were marched down a long corridor to the probation office. Karen stood stiffly, like a soldier at attention. Tyler slumped and stared at the floor. He didn't care what the police or probation officers did to him anymore. He just wanted to go home and sleep.

"The charges against him are really pretty minor," the probation officer told Karen. "And since he's never been arrested before, we'll probably just assign him some consequences through this department rather than taking it through court. I can tell you now that he'll need to do some community service. Does he see a therapist?"

"Yes," Karen replied. "I already have an emergency appointment set up for him for Monday morning. I just don't know what got into him. He's had his bad days before but never like this."

The probation officer frowned and inspected Tyler's face closely. "Tyler, can you tell me what got you so upset?"

Tyler shrugged and looked away.

"We had a younger boy leave earlier in the day to go to his adoptive home," Karen offered. "He and Tyler were very close."

"That's not it," Tyler interjected quickly. He couldn't understand why people just couldn't mind their own business.

"What was it then?" Karen asked curtly.

"I don't know."

The probation officer sniffed and began to scrawl some notes on the bottom of a very official-looking form. "Well, maybe your therapist can help you figure out where that anger's coming from," he said gently. "Of course we don't want to see you doing this kind of stuff again. As you get older, or if you continue to behave aggressively and destroy other people's property, it'll get more serious and the consequences will get worse. Do you understand that?"

"Yes," Tyler said. In his head, he was screaming: Shut up! Shut up! Shut up! God, what do I have to do to stop getting lectures from all of you?

"Okay. I'm going to assign you twenty-five hours of community service work, Tyler. That means you have to volunteer your time to help the community. Doing chores around your house doesn't count. You can help out a neighbor or a teacher or contact an organization in town which might take young volunteers, okay? You need to have all twenty-five hours completed in two months time."

He handed the form to Karen and wished them a good morning.

The ride home was quiet and uncomfortable, with Karen saying nothing to him other than to tell him he was grounded to the house until further notice. And as promised, first thing on Monday morning she drove him to Dr. Cardenas's office so he could discuss the episode with a trained professional. That particular day, Dr. Cardenas had again forgotten his name again and referred to him consistently as "Tom." By the end of the session, Dr. Cardenas had also concluded it was Sawyer's departure from the lighthouse which had induced the fit of rage. Tyler didn't bother to argue with him. He knew the emotions still boiling in him were coming from some other place entirely.

CHAPTER THIRTEEN

Tyler remained confined to the lighthouse for the remainder of the week, allowed outside its walls only to attend school or complete the impressive list of chores and yard work Karen had compiled for him. By the following Friday he had redeemed himself enough that he was allowed to phone Captain Spolarich.

"For Pete's sake," the old man chuckled, "I thought you'd forgotten all about me, Tyler."

"No," the boy replied sheepishly. "I got in trouble. I've been grounded for the last week."

"Oh, dear. I'm sorry to hear that."

"Were you able to find any photos of Ehren Tschantz?"

"I found a whole stack of stuff on Ehren Tschantz, my friend. Maybe you and I need to get together again?"

"Ummm, yeah, I was wondering about that actually. I'm supposed to do something nice for an old person, you see..."

The Captain paused. "Sorry, I'm not following you."

Tyler cringed. His mouth always sunk him. "I mean, well, I got in trouble and that's why I was grounded. I kind of made a mess in my mom's house so the police came and now they want me to do twenty-five hours to help someone out... Since you're old, I mean, since you're an older person than me I was wondering if maybe you needed something done around your house? It's all for free. I could rake the leaves in your yard or something and then maybe you could show me the photos too?"

The Captain chuckled at Tyler's clumsiness. "You know I don't see very well out of this one eye of mine," he said, "so it's hard for me to do things around this old place. I'm sure I could come up with a few things for you to do. If you do good work, maybe we can even turn it into a paying job. What do you think?"

Tyler smiled, perhaps for the first time in seven days. "Okay," he answered, "I'll talk to my mom about it and then call you back."

Karen had no concerns about Tyler's arrangement with Captain Spolarich and even liked the symmetry of him cleaning up an old man's house as penance for having destroyed part of his own. Griffin agreed to drive him to the town where Captain Spolarich lived in a pale yellow two-story house with a large elm tree in the front yard. It was obvious from first glance the Captain might have needed more assistance than Tyler first imagined. The old man was clearly a collector of things. Not of particular things, but of things in general. The yard was curiously decorated with a weathered collection of lawn ornaments including ceramic frogs, broken fountains and a small herd of iron deer statues which for some reason had been buried up to their flanks in the ground. The long porch had a large American flag draped from its rafters and was cluttered with gardening tools, flower pots and dozens of wood boxes filled to the rim with rusted horseshoes, seashells and antique bottles. Milling about, often hidden in the nooks and crannies between the clutter, were half-dozen cats, each decorated with a bright nylon collar and a small brass bell.

Griffin looked upon the clutter with amusement. "Dude, you have soooo much work to do," he snickered.

"Shut up," Tyler whispered. "These are probably all his treasures."

"Yeah, this's a bunch of junk. He's probably one of those old weird guys who has stacks of newspapers dating back fifty years piled in his living room."

Tyler ignored him and rang the door bell. The sound was immediately answered by the soft mewing of more cats inside.

"Who's there?" Captain Spolarich called.

"Captain, it's me Tyler. I'm here with my brother, Griff."

It took nearly a minute for the old man to toddle to the front door. As the boys entered the living room they understood why. The interior of the house was even more cluttered than the yard, with only a narrow pathway between the ottoman, the various tables and bureaus, and the piles of statues, paintings, pottery and curios.

"Wow, you got a lot of stuff, Captain," Tyler said, bluntly.

It's all my artwork, my boy," Captain Spolarich answered. "Life's too short not to have beautiful things around you."

"Do you have big piles of old newspapers too?" Tyler asked instantly.

Griffin gawked at him.

"Why? Do you need old newspapers?"

Tyler struggled to correct himself. "Naw. Just wondering."

Griffin interrupted. "Captain Spolarich, I'll just leave Tyler with you if that's okay and then be back in a couple of hours to get him?"

"Fine, fine... I'll keep him busy."

Once Griffin had departed, the Captain turned to Tyler and said, "I owe you an apology."

This might be a first, Tyler mused. Someone is apologizing to me instead of the other way 'round?

Now that the Captain had promised an apology, Tyler wondered what form it would take. He was familiar with all of them, having spent so much of his life issuing apologies. Would it be in written form, as seemed to be the preferred method in the public school system? Or would it be the long, detailed account of every dishonest moment the Captain had had for the past month, which was the method preferred by Dr. Cardenas? Or would it be accompanied by days of boring work in which the guilty would have to clean out gutters or scrub toilet bowls as was Karen's favorite tactic?

"Why do you owe me an apology?" Tyler asked.

"I lied to you, young man," the Captain said stiffly.

An apology and a confession to a lie, all in one day? Tyler felt like he'd landed in an alternate dimension.

Captain Spolarich continued: "When I met you and your brother for lunch, I told you that I didn't know what had happened to any of the eight Germans who'd been in the barracks the night Ehren Tschantz was killed. Well, that wasn't completely true. I didn't know what happened to most of them, but there were a couple I... well... tracked through the years."

"Why?"

"All of the men in that dormitory had conspired to either kill Ehren or hide the murderers after the crime was committed. We knew that from day one, but we were never able to identify the men who actually held the pillow over his face and killed him. But I still had my prime suspects, you know? There were two in particular I thought knew more than the rest."

He gestured for Tyler to follow and hobbled his way up the stairs and through the maze-like house he'd inhabited for the past fifty years. They finally ended up in a small bedroom where nearly every inch of wall-space was occupied by a framed photo, certificate, poster, newspaper clipping or war medal. Along the walls were a variety of mismatched tables stacked with cardboard boxes stuffed with documents and filing cabinets overflowing with rumpled papers. For Tyler, it was like stepping through a time portal into a part of Captain Spolarich's past dedicated to his military service. Many of the items nailed to the walls were of a personal nature, such as yellowing photos of the Captain at a time when he was young, healthy and had a full head of hair. There was a photo of him leaning against a silver jet on the deck of an aircraft carrier. There was another of him shaking hands with a stately-looking man in a dark uniform heavily trimmed with fancy braid. There was a tattered American flag neatly folded and placed inside a triangular glass box. There were photographs, some in muted color, of various battleships, cruisers and cutters. And there was an entire corner dedicated to Ehren Tschantz.

Tyler recognized some of the images he and Ms. Trease had downloaded from the internet almost immediately. One newspaper headline which read DEATH OF P.O.W. AT FT. MEADE UNDER INVESTIGATION was the same article they'd found after his return from Maryland. It seemed like the Captain had just escorted him into a private shrine, something which made Tyler feel both honored and uneasy.

"As you can see," the Captain said, pointing to the wall with his rosewood cane, "I may have lied to you more than I thought."

Tyler didn't respond. He began to run his fingers over the materials spread out on the table near the wall. Among the jumble of books and file folders were a variety of mismatched items, including a pocket watch, a hair brush, a sterling silver ring and several old color photographs which had been cut out of magazines. Tyler lifted the photos gingerly and thumbed through them. The strangest sensation began to draw over him, a feeling of familiarity and loss. It reminded him of when he tried to remember his mother, someone he hadn't seen in years and whose memory had become more of a vague feeling in the pit of his stomach. The photos he held, all of the rocky and beautiful New England coast, inspired the same reaction. He set the photos carefully on the table top and moved onto a stack of small pastel drawings, quaint artistic studies of a bird sitting in a tree, rain clouds over a rooftop and snow falling in the moonlight. That weird feeling grew and Captain Spolarich seemed to sense it.

"What do you think about those pictures?" the old man asked kindly.

Tyler shrugged. He didn't know how to describe what he was feeling so he said nothing.

"Take a look here," the Captain said, tapping the wall nearby with the tip of his cane.

Tyler drew closer to the wall and inspected an old photograph of about ten men, all dressed in heavy denim overalls and cotton shirts, who were filing down a ship's gangplank. Most were in bare feet. A few had scraggly beards. One was smiling, a big toothy grin like he was on shore-leave and didn't have a care in the world. He had dark hair, a square head, a strong jaw and a long straight nose which made him look like a piece of Classical sculpture. Although the photo was black and white, Tyler could tell he had blue eyes.

"Who is this man?" Tyler asked.

"You tell me, Tyler," the Captain replied. "Who is he?"

Tyler straightened and frowned. "How should I know? I've never seen him before in my life."

"Look at him closer," the Captain urged.

The man's large blue eyes stirred images in Tyler's head which seemed completely foreign, as though they were thoughts belonging to someone else entirely. Blue. Blue like the ocean at high noon on a clear day. Blue like the flowers which covered the hillsides in spring. So blue this young man's mother had complimented him on them almost every day, telling him she could see his very soul dancing across their surface.

"It's Tschantz," Tyler stated, almost unthinkingly.

"No," the Captain said. "Look again. You know this answer."

Tyler concentrated. He studied the man from the shape of his ears to the curve of his shoulders. As he stood there staring at the photo, another face, a different face began to peer back at him. The face was younger with dark, sad eyes and a long, slender shape topped by a mass of unruly hair.

Tyler let out a sharp gasp and turned to face the old man.

Captain Spolarich was smiling curiously at him. "I didn't know for sure when I first met you," he said. "There was something familiar about you, something about your mannerisms, how you spoke... Something about how angry and determined you were at the same time. I didn't know what it was, but I couldn't sleep that night thinking I knew you from somewhere else. But believe it or not, I don't pal around with a lot of teenagers so I was growing more and more frustrated trying to figure it out."

Tyler stood frozen. It suddenly occurred to him that the old man had used the same technique on him he'd tried on Sawyer to jog those memories from a past life. Tyler had taken Sawyer to an old graveyard. Captain Spolarich had laid out a collection of mementos and waited to see which Tyler would pick up. Tyler remembered the story Ms. Trease had read to him, about the young Sri Lankan girl who remembered a former life as a boy. The boy's family had tested her in this same way, hadn't they? Suddenly, Tyler felt duped.

The Captain shuffled over to a chair and sat down, hanging his cane on the corner of a nearby table covered with mounds of books, photo albums and storage boxes. He pulled an album onto his lap and flipped through the stiff black pages.

"I wasn't convinced until just now, however," he said, "when I saw your face as you were looking at those pastel drawings. At the drawings you made."

Tyler glanced down at the illustrations he was still clutching in his hands. "I didn't draw these. I can't draw at all," he said. But he said so without fully believing it. There was something about the feel of the paper and the pattern of the chalky strokes which made a shiver run up his back.

"I know this seems so impossible, but isn't this the answer you came here to find?" the Captain asked. "I told you that I didn't know what had happened to the men in that dorm room when Ehren was killed, and I thought it was a pretty impressive lie. I thought I sounded very convincing, but you didn't want to let it go. I knew right then that this wasn't about some writing assignment for school."

"It is for school," Tyler said automatically.

"Hell's bells," Captain Spolarich chortled, "kids don't do this much investigating for a simple school assignment, my friend. They steal a few paragraphs out of an encyclopedia and sign their name to it. You're either the best darn student in New England or your interest is much more personal. And I'm guessing you're not much of a student, am I right?"

"I'm not a good student," Tyler confessed. "I'm not even a very good person."

Captain Spolarich snorted. "Now, I didn't say anything about you not being a good person. You seem to be a very good person. You're certainly a driven person. Driven... like him..." He pointed to the photo of the smiling Tschantz. "All those years ago, you would set your mind to something and not let go of it. You kept fighting the Nazis, in your own way, right up to the very end. Do you remember that?"

"No. I'm not Tschantz. This little boy I live with, well, used to live with, he's a foster kid like me and I think it was him because he knew all this stuff about U-boats. He knew things he shouldn't know 'cause he was so young and I think it was him —"

"—and I think it was you!" Captain Spolarich said resolutely.

"No. It's Sawyer, the little boy I used to live with."

"Tyler, if this is all about somebody else, why are you so obsessed with it? This child doesn't even live with you anymore, but here you are, still trying to discover the truth about his past. Maybe the reason you're so interested is because it's always been about you?"

Tyler wasn't able to answer. This was in fact a question he'd avoided asking ever since these thoughts began to occur to him so many weeks before. It'd been so much easier, perhaps less crazy-sounding, to believe Sawyer was the one with the connection to the shadowy German sailor. Could he have been wrong all along?

"This is crazy," Tyler said.

"It's your quest, my friend," the Captain said. "Don't turn away now that you're getting some answers. I know it's you. Even with my bad eyesight, I can see Ehren Tschantz inside you."

A jolt like cold electricity crackled in Tyler's brain. "I better go," he said quickly. "I'll wait for my brother outside."

"You just got here."

"I know, but I got to go now."

"Tyler!" the Captain called as the boy moved hurriedly toward the door.

"Yeah?"

"I told you a lie when I first met you. I told you I didn't know what happened to the eight men who were in that dorm room with you on the evening of January 17th, 1945. But there were two I've been watching for years. I couldn't forget what they'd done to you. I couldn't let go of it so I've spent the last sixty-plus years keeping tabs on them."

"So?" Tyler asked. "Get to the point. I want to leave."

"Tyler, after the war was over, one man returned to Germany and died there about fifteen years ago. But the other one emigrated to the United States after the war. He's the one who I felt right from the beginning orchestrated your murder. Tyler, he's alive and I know where he is."

CHAPTER FOURTEEN

It took Tyler the full week before he was ready to even entertain the thought of returning to Captain Spolarich's house for another day of community service. He had seriously considered never returning and had even ignored the Captain's phone calls for a while. But as the days passed and Tyler had more time to digest what he'd been feeling all along, the notion that it was he — not Sawyer — who was the reincarnated soul of Ehren Tschantz seemed less impossible. Or at least it seemed no more impossible than the idea of reincarnation itself.

Finally, one night he crept up to Griffin's room and sitting in the hammock, swinging back and forth as an Atlantic gale beat against the lighthouse walls, he told the boy he considered his brother absolutely everything. To his surprise, Griffin's reaction was one of relief.

"Do you think that's crazy?" Tyler asked.

"Tyler, I've known you for all these years and I've never seen you behave like you have in the past few weeks. And I gotta be honest, this thought has crossed my mind before."

"Why?"

"Because the more I thought about some of the things that happened to Sawyer, the more it seemed like they were really happening to you. Remember, one of the first things you said to me was that Sawyer had some strange word for submarine."

"Right. Unterseeboot."

"Yeah, but what if he was just saying "under sea boat?" If you're an eight-year-old, you might just call a submarine an 'under sea boat?' It's just a simple way for a child to describe what he's seeing. It was you who knew the word unterseeboot, not Sawyer."

Tyler groaned. "Was it?"

"Think about this for a sec, dude. I never really heard Sawyer express any interest in U-boats or World War II or German sailors. He was just a little dude who thought submarines were cool. But his interest really seemed to trigger your brain. I mean — dude — you started hanging out in the school library!"

Tyler was quiet, lost in his thoughts.

"I have a question for you," Griffin continued.

"Yeah?"

"When we were in the graveyard at Fort Meade, why did you take those photos of Ehren Tschantz's grave?"

"Because Sawyer was freaking out when he saw it."

"No, he wasn't."

"Yes he was, Griff."

"No, he wasn't. Tyler, he was freaking out because he's eight years old and we took him to a cemetery. Any eight-year-old would probably react like that."

"I guess."

"So answer my question. Why did you photograph Ehren Tschantz's grave? Of all the graves in that cemetery, why that one?"

"I don't really know. It had a German name on it, I guess."

"There were others right next to it with German names. You didn't photograph those."

Again Tyler didn't answer. More correctly, he couldn't answer. Suddenly he began to wonder how many other incidents he had, which at the time seemed irrelevant or just coincidental, but were now much more meaningful than he thought. Why, for example, had he wondered if there was a video camera hidden in the overhead lamp at the juvenile detention center? Did that mean anything?

Tyler never tried to explain to himself how reincarnation might happen. All those scientists who'd investigated it for decades still had nothing but theories, so it was unlikely that he, a thirteen-year-old with uniformly poor grades, would be able to explain something which seemed as much a matter of faith as anything else. Perhaps it was more important to just feel it.

"Griff," he asked after a few moments of deep reflection, "if it's me, why do you think this would happen now?"

Griffin pursed his lips and said slowly, "Those books and websites you were reading about reincarnation, they all said that many people who remember their past lives start out with one incident. They see or hear or experience something and — boom — it's like a door suddenly opens."

"Right. It's called a 'trigger event.'"

"Well, what if Sawyer was your trigger? What if his constant babbling about submarines was just enough to jog those memories for you?"

"I guess that's kind of how it happened."

"There must be something to this, Tyler. Ever since he came into the house, you've behaved like a completely different person. You are so... well, I don't even know how to describe it..."

"The Captain said I was 'driven,' whatever that means."

"It means that he's seeing the same thing I'm seeing. You've never been more interested in anything in your life than you've been in this dead German sailor. If Captain Spolarich came to this same conclusion after talking to you only a few times, there must be something about you that reminded him of Tschantz — something you weren't even aware of."

"What should I do?" Tyler asked, suddenly feeling crestfallen. Wasn't his own life troubled enough without having the shoulder one belonging to a man who'd died decades earlier?

"What do you want to do? Or wait, let me ask that in a different way. What would Ehren Tschantz want you to do?"

He didn't need to think long about the answer. "Captain Spolarich says he knows where one of the murderer is, that he's living in America now."

Griffin was surprised. "He's still alive? He must be ancient."

"Captain Spolarich is still alive."

"Well, barely."

"Shut up, Griff. Don't be so mean."

"I'm not trying to be mean, dude, I'm just surprised any of these guys are still around and kicking. How does Spolarich know where he is?"

"I'm not really sure. He just said he had two main suspects and he's been tracking them over the years."

"Are you thinking of trying to find this man, this potential murderer?"

Tyler shrugged.

"I guess I don't have to tell you how crazy dangerous that would be?"

"Why? He wouldn't know me, right? I'm just some dumb kid."

"Tyler..."

"Griff, you just asked me what Ehren Tschantz wants of me. Maybe this is what he wants? Whoever murdered me all those years ago got away with it."

"What! What did you just say? Did you hear yourself?"

"Huh?"

"You just said 'whoever murdered me got away with it.' Me. You said 'me' instead of 'him.'"

"No, I said 'him.' Whoever killed Ehren got away with it."

"You didn't say that, Tyler."

"Well, then it was just a slip of the tongue. Why are you being so weird about it?"

"Because that's what I've been saying to you all this time," Griffin sighed. "This is about you. And you want revenge!"

Tyler thought about it for a moment and then replied, "Maybe I just want justice?"

On Saturday, Griffin and Tyler returned to the cluttered yellow house and found Captain Spolarich sitting in an overstuffed recliner decorated with cats. Across the room, the television was softly humming with the voices on an old black-and-white movie.

"C'mon in, boys," the old man yelled. The cats stirred as Griffin and Tyler entered, although most just rose, stretched, turned and lay down again. "I'd get up but it would disturb the masters of the house," he chuckled. "Welcome back."

"Thanks," Tyler said. "Is it okay if Griff stays today?"

The Captain looked perplexed.

"I know all about it," Griffin added.

"It? What's 'it?'"

"About what you said to Tyler the last time he was here. He told me everything."

The Captain didn't reply. Years of work as an interrogator had taught him not to speak unless you needed to, especially if someone else was willing to do it for you.

Griffin cleared his throat and stated firmly, "I know all about Ehren Tschantz and I want to help."

"Do you now?"

"Yes, sir."

"And you don't think your brother and I are just a little loopy?"

Griffin laughed. "Life's filled with crazy stuff I guess."

"True enough," the Captain agreed.

Then, as if to underscore that thought, the movie the old man was watching suddenly crackled with trumpets blasting triumphantly. The shot tightened on a large poster depicting the American bald eagle ripping apart a Japanese flag with its talons. Above the eagle's wings were the words REMEMBER PEARL HARBOR! The fanfare faded to the husky voice of a young woman. Tyler found himself settling onto the couch to watch. The woman, wearing the uniform of the American Red Cross, was delivering a speech before an auditorium of men representing the various branches of the United States military. She spoke with great authority and purpose, her small mouth carefully outlined in dark lipstick and her huge eyes flashing behind the funny-looking round glasses. The speech the woman gave was passionate and patriotic and much longer than something Tyler would typically sit and listen to, but he found him completely absorbed. He began to mimic her words with no more presence of mind than someone who hummed along to a familiar tune while riding an elevator.

When the scene ended, he turned toward Griffin and Captain Spolarich. Both were staring incredulously at him.

"What was that?" Griffin laughed. But Captain Spolarich was silent.

"What's the matter?" Tyler asked him.

"Tyler, how'd you do that?" the old man asked. "How'd you know the lines from that movie?"

"That lady, the actress... I was just copying her."

"I know that, son, but you were saying those words like you knew them by heart. How'd you know the words that lady was saying as she said them?"

The Captain's tone and expression made Tyler shiver. Griffin suddenly understood the oddness of the situation. "Why?" he asked. "What does it mean?"

"Shh! Shh!" Captain Spolarich snapped. He wasn't angry, just anxious. "Let him remember on his own."

They waited silently. Tyler felt like one of those times in class when his teacher made him come up to the board and solve a math problem in front of everyone. He hated that kind of pressure. Usually he'd just evade the situation by printing FART in big letters on the board and receiving an immediate referral to the assistant principal's office, but that option didn't exist in this case. Tyler looked back at the movie. The scene had changed and the beautiful actress was now dressed in a large fur stole and an elegant evening gown and was sitting in a nightclub across from a man wearing a U.S. Army uniform. Was she familiar somehow, he asked himself? Was there something about her eyes which Tyler recognized but couldn't place?

Finally he just replied, "I don't know."

The Captain looked disappointed.

"Did you set me up again?" Tyler asked. "Was this another test?"

The old man looked sheepish and nodded. "I guess I did," he confessed. "In December 1944, just before Christmas, I drove Ehren Tschantz into Baltimore and took him to the cinema. It was a big, big risk. If my bosses had ever found out I'd done that, they probably would have put me in prison for certain. But it was my Christmas present to Ehren... one night of freedom, to feel like a real person rather than just a prisoner. The motion picture we saw that night was this one. I don't suppose you can remember the name of the film?"

Both boys looked back at the screen.

Tyler shook his head. "I don't know. I'm sorry."

Captain Spolarich smiled kindly. "It's called 'Old Acquaintance,'" he said and then chuckled. "I just realized how that title is so appropriate for our situation, Tyler. We are, after all, old acquaintances."

"Are you saying that Tyler — I'm mean Ehren — saw this same film with you all those years ago?" Griffin asked.

"That's what I'm saying. But at that time, the movie was brand new. I remember you were quite in love with Bette Davis."

Tyler looked back at the screen and pointed to the woman with the large eyes. "That's her, right?" he asked, although he didn't know why he would assume this. He had never heard of anyone named Bette Davis.

"That's right," the Captain replied. "I'm not trying to trick you or anything. I guess I just needed a little more reassurance, and I think you gave it to me." He gently roused the cats which were clustered around his waist and shoulders and balanced himself against his rosewood cane. He looked at Griffin and asked, "Do you drive, young man?"

"Yes, sir."

"And you have your car with you?"

"Yes."

"Well, good," he announced, "we should go. We have a long drive ahead of us."

"I'm supposed to do some work for you," Tyler said anxiously. "I need to complete my twenty-five hours for the probation officer."

"Yes, yes, yes... All right. Today you mowed my lawn, weeded my garden and swept my porch. That should be good for about six hours. How does that sound?" the Captain asked with a wink.

Tyler smiled and nodded.

The Captain provided Griffin with directions and they began a meandering journey along tree-lined country roads and through quaint New England hamlets filled with clapboard houses and towering churches with elegant spires and shimmering stained-glass windows. Autumn was just beginning to encroach on the landscape, tinting the leaves with mustard yellow and burnt orange. It was the time of year Captain Spolarich liked best, and as he watched the landscape streak by he felt something he hadn't felt in years — elation. He'd retired from the military with a tarnished reputation. He'd married only to see his wife succumb at an early age to cancer, leaving him with no children and a large, empty house he had tried to fill with beautiful things and which now sat as dust-covered clutter. His best friends had proven to be his cats, and although they were warm and comforting, the conversation left much to be desired. He'd felt for years that his life was defined by missed opportunities and unfinished business. But now, by some twist of fate he didn't understand and was hesitant to question, one of the greatest regrets of his life seemed possible to correct. He studied the back of Tyler's head, squinting with his one good eye at the long tip of the boy's jaw and the curve of his small ears. He certainly looked nothing like Ehren Tschantz, but the more he was with Tyler the more he felt both a sense of familiarity and compassion. He didn't know what had happened to the boy to land him in foster care and he decided early on not to ask. Whatever it was, it seemed universally unfair one soul should suffer so much over two separate lifetimes. The excitement he felt had a lot to do with correcting this cosmic mistake as well.

After a little more than an hour, they came to a small village which lay just inside the New York state border, overlooking the broad gray swath of the Hudson River. The town had been constructed along the sloping banks, so the streets were steep and narrow. It was obvious from Captain Spolarich's directions that he knew exactly where he wanted to go, although their progress was hampered by his poor eyesight. He finally directed Griffin to turn into a small empty parking lot which bordered a squat brown building with a peaked roof trimmed with wooden scrollwork. A large hand-painted sign was hung above the entrance and read THE HEIDELBERG CLUB.

"What's this?" Tyler asked.

"This's where we find the man I believe killed Ehren Tschantz," the Captain replied.

"But what is it?"

"It's a German-American club. People with German ancestry come here to socialize or listen to music or have parties. He owns the place. He's owned it for years. It's made him a very rich man."

Griffin was irritated. "So this dude kills Ehren Tschantz, gets away with it and comes back later to open a club and earn a fortune?"

"Keep in mind, son, this man was never convicted of anything. In the eyes of the law and the U.S. government, he's not a criminal at all. After the war, he returned to Germany and then in the late 1960s he and his wife emigrated back to the U.S. By that time, whatever happened in the P.O.W. dormitory at Fort Meade was old news, forgotten by everyone except me. And maybe him."

"How do you know all this?" Tyler asked.

"After I retired from the Navy, I kept in contact with some of my friends who were still in the intelligence business. They fed me details about him from time to time. When he relocated back to the United States, it became easier to watch him. Once he opened this club, it became easier still. They have a nice website."

"Geeze, dude," groaned Griffin, "you're like a stalker or something."

"Hmm. Perhaps you would think differently if he'd murdered one of your friends," the Captain responded tersely.

Rebuked, Griffin elected not to say anything else.

"What should we do?" Tyler wondered.

"I think you need to see him," the Captain said. "You need to lay eyes on him and see if it jogs anything loose." He handed Tyler a neatly folded slip of paper upon which was written the name ACHIM JUNGCLAUS.

"This's him?" Tyler asked.

"That's him."

"Do I just go up to the door and ask for him."

"That's what I'd do."

"Then what do I do?"

"Talk to him, I guess. Ask him some questions. Ask him about the club."

"Are you guys coming?"

"I don't think we should," the Captain responded.

"What if he's dangerous?" Griffin protested.

Tyler grinned roguishly and answered, "Griff, remember he doesn't know me. I'm just some stupid kid. It'll be fine."

Tyler opened the car door and stepped onto the pavement. As he walked across to the building he could smell the aroma of cooking sausages and hear the low timbre of German music playing somewhere inside. The main entrance led into an large enclosed courtyard lined with wooden benches and surrounded by flower boxes. At the far end was a wooden stage over which was hung a vinyl banner announcing the impending Oktoberfest celebration. There didn't appear to be anyone in the courtyard, although the sounds of music and laughter were now closer and louder. Tyler stood there for a long moment, wondering what he should do next. His thoughts were interrupted when an elegant woman in her mid-70s wandered out from one of the adjoining doorways. She looked curiously at him and then smiled.

"Hello there," she said. Her voice was gentle but colored with a pronounced German accent. "Can I help you with something?"

Tyler crumpled the note Captain Spolarich had given him and concealed it in the palm of his hand. Suddenly his heart was thumping like he'd just run a mile. "Is the owner here?" he asked.

The woman raised an eyebrow. "I'm the owner," she said. "What can I do for you?"

Oops, he thought. She must be the wife. Well, no where to go but forward. "Umm, I was wondering how someone joins your club?"

"Are you interested in joining, young man?"

"Yes. But I don't think I'm German."

She laughed. "It's not required that you're German, but we don't accept children unless their mom or dad are members."

"Oh," he said dejectedly and turned to leave.

"Wait a moment," she called. He stopped and turned to face her. "Why are you interested in joining?"

"Umm," he thought for a moment and decided to fall back on a time-tested excuse, "I'm doing some research for school."

"Oh! You must be studying world cultures, yes? We've had some other boys and girls come by for that before."

"Yes," Tyler nodded.

She was about to reply when a man appeared from the same doorway and called to her. He was large, robust and as bald as a baby. He had an immense white mustache which hid his entire mouth except for the lower lip. Although he appeared to be close to Spolarich's age, he wasn't the bent and fragile figure the Captain was. As he walked across the courtyard toward them, he moved with the hulking gait of a rhinoceros. There was no question in Tyler's mind as to who he was.

"Are you coming back inside?" he asked the woman.

"Yes, dear," she replied. "I was just speaking to this young man. He's doing some research on Germany for school. He wants to join the club."

"I'm sorry," Jungclaus said, "but we don't allow children to join."

"I already told him, dear," Mrs. Jungclaus interjected. "However — oh, I'm sorry — I didn't catch your name..."

Tyler thought frantically for a moment. He felt like a cat burglar who had just been discovered standing next to a priceless artifact with his bag wide open. He knew his anxiety was irrational. This couple saw him as nothing more than what he was — a tongue-tied teenager with messy hair. He rolled the crumbled slip of paper in his fingers and answered awkwardly, "My name is Ehren."

"Very nice to meet you, Aaron," Mrs. Jungclaus replied. "I was going to suggest you come back for Oktoberfest" — she gestured to the banner over the wooden stage — "it's open to the public and you can get an excellent taste of authentic German food and music. How does that sound?"

Jungclaus nodded his approval. The introduction of the name Ehren had clearly gone unnoticed by the great hulk of a man. Tyler didn't know what he'd hoped to accomplish by letting the name slip, but clearly it'd been ineffectual. "That'd be a perfect solution," Jungclaus said.

Tyler found he couldn't take his eyes off of him, and it was his nervousness which finally made the large German shift his weight uneasily and clear his throat. "Will that help you?" he asked.

Tyler nodded slightly. "Yes," he replied. "I'll come back. Thank you."

He turned and walked swiftly for the exit, not bothering to look back until he'd reached the parking lot and suddenly noticed the balled scrap of paper was no longer in his hand. His eyes flashed over the ground but it was no where to be seen. Had he dropped it inside? He didn't dare to return, but stood frozen for a moment just staring at the club's entrance. Then Griffin honked the car horn. Tyler ran back to where he and Captain Spolarich were waiting.

"What were you doing?" Griffin asked.

"Nothing, nothing," Tyler said.

"Did you see him?" Captain Spolarich asked eagerly.

"Yes."

"And?"

"And I don't know... I talked to him and his wife briefly. They were very nice. Can we leave?"

Griffin shrugged and started the car. As they drove out of the parking lot, Tyler glanced back at the Heidelberg Club. Achim Jungclaus had appeared in the doorway, holding a scrap of crumpled paper in his fingers, and stood there watching them until the car had driven out of sight.

.

CHAPTER FIFTEEN

The Heidelberg Club was trimmed with ribbons and colorful pennants in black, bright gold and deep red. They were the same colors Tyler had seen decorating the German graves in the Fort Meade cemetery, the colors of a democratic nation which had pulled itself out of the ruins of the Second World War and had joined its old enemies as a new friend. They were different colors from the ones Captain Spolarich had come to associate with Germany. For so long he had remembered only the blood red of the Nazi flag with the sinister swastika in the middle. Seeing the emblems of a new Germany snapping in the wind over the club's gabled roof filled the Captain with a certain sense of pride. It also reminded him there was a criminal hiding behind those peaceful colors.

Had there been any speculation about the financial success of Achim Jungclaus and the Heidelberg Club, it faded as Tyler and his two companions wound their way through the club's parking lot which was filled with a mass of laughing people, concession booths, carnival games and folk musicians. A man with a harmonica in his mouth, a large drum on his belly and brass cymbals on his knees tipped his green felt hat to the boys as they entered and launched into a thunderous refrain. Women with their hair tied into tight braids and wearing short skirts embroidered with wild flowers spun through the crowd while effortlessly balancing trays loaded with beer steins. Tyler paused briefly to watch a caricature artist sketch a young girl in pastel chalk before Griffin caught his elbow and coaxed him along.

"Keep up or we'll lose the Captain in this crowd," he said.

The truth be told, it was unlikely either boy could have misplaced the old man for long. He'd dressed very deliberately for this day... and more garishly than usual. His bright yellow WORLD WAR II VETERAN hat sat lopsided on his head and he was wearing an oversized grey sweatshirt emblazoned with a large American flag, baggy khaki trousers and red socks with leather sandals. While Tyler had long thought the old man's unusual wardrobe choices were the result of carelessness, today seemed different. Clearly, the Captain wanted to be seen and this concerned Tyler. He and Griffin had chauffeured the Captain back to upstate New York thinking their mission would be simple: sit in the crowd and observe Achim Jungclaus from a distance. Now Tyler wasn't so sure this was Captain Spolarich's intention. Indeed, the old man seemed to be on a crusade, pointing his way through the ocean of people with his rosewood cane and leading them deep into the club's courtyard.

"Do you know where you're going, Captain?" Griffin asked.

The old man didn't respond, but stood for a moment in the entrance while he surveyed the crowd inside. He pointed with the tip of his cane, almost knocking the hat off a woman's head, and announced loudly, "There we go!"

He led the boys across to an open table located just to the right of the main stage. He lowered himself into a chair and hung the cane on the end of the table.

"What now?" Tyler asked.

"Now we wait," the Captain smiled.

"For what?"

"For him."

The boys sat down quickly and Griffin leaned in close to Spolarich. "How do you know he'll even be here, Captain?"

"Of course he'll be here. He's German. It's Oktoberfest. He owns the club. Where else would he be?"

Then, with a patience only years of practice could perfect, the old man leaned back, folded his arms and sat quietly. Over the next hour, a variety of performers took the stage with acts ranging from dance routines to stand-up comedy, but nothing moved the Captain from his spot. Finally, after what had seemed like an eternity to Tyler and Griffin, Achim Jungclaus ascended the stage and basked in the cheers of the crowd. Clearly, in this place and at this time, he was a much beloved man. He held his hands high over his head and the cheers diminished. He tapped the microphone with a meaty finger.

"Can you hear me?" he boomed over the loud speakers.

"Ja!" the crowd responded in thunderous harmony.

"Are you enjoying our Oktoberfest celebration?" Jungclaus grinned.

"Ja!" the crowd responded.

"Are you ready for more?"

"JA! JA! JA!"

He was handed a large tankard of beer by his wife, the same dignified-looking lady Tyler had spoken to earlier in the month, and raised it to the crowd. "A toast!" he proclaimed. A hundred hands shot into the air, holding aloft steins, bottles and soda cans. "To all of you, for joining me and my family on this beautiful autumn day for this year's Oktoberfest. To Germany, our homeland! And to America, our home!"

The audience rolled with cheers and the clinking of glass against glass. Jungclaus waited patiently for the noise to abate, but before he could utter another word,

Captain Spolarich had clumsily climbed onto his chair and was waving his cane in the air.

Tyler suddenly felt his body seize up with fear. Oh no, he thought, what's he up to?

The Captain raised the beer stein he had been nursing and bellowed, "Another toast..."

Jungclaus was staring at him with a combination of amusement and befuddlement, but there was no hostility there. After all, he was just an old man and probably half-drunk to boot.

Captain Spolarich turned and tipped his stein toward Jungclaus. "Let's toast our magnanimous host!" he called to a smattering of hesitant applause. "To Leutnant zur See Achim Jungclaus, the pride of the Kreigsmarine who in 1945, along with seven other men, smothered an unarmed and defenseless boy in his own bed because they thought him a spy! To you, Leutnant zur See Jungclaus, a murderer and coward!"

Although the music and voices from the parking lot continued uninterrupted, the crowd inside the courtyard had fallen deathly silent. Tyler glanced around in a panic. Most of the faces looking back were confused and annoyed that the party had suddenly come to a crashing halt.

After a few seconds of staring unblinkingly at Spolarich, Jungclaus appeared to collect himself and chuckled into the microphone, "We have a three beer maximum here, sir."

The audience chortled, but it was uncomfortable and insincere. Captain Spolarich, who'd been teetering on the chair, almost fell as he made a futile jab at the hulking German with his cane. Griffin grabbed the old man and steadied him.

"That's enough, Captain," he whispered urgently. "I think we just outstayed our welcome here."

But Captain Spolarich ignored him, having waited so long for this confrontation. He bellowed, "Hands off me, boy!" He turned back to the assembly and gestured again at Jungclaus. "You see, he doesn't think anyone remembers. He thinks he got away with it and that time would forgive his crime. But I remember it! And what's more —" he pointed to Tyler with the cane "— he remembers it!"

Jungclaus, whose wife was now anxiously clinging to his arm, glanced down at Tyler. "He remembers what?" the man asked calmly. There was a sudden silence in the room. The entire audience was now curious. What did the teenaged boy, whose face was bright red with embarrassment, remember?

"He remembers what you did, you scoundrel!" Spolarich cried. "You killed his body, but Fate had a different goal and his spirit survived! He is Ehren Tschantz, the man you murdered in 1945 in the P.O.W. dormitory at Fort Meade, Maryland!"

Captain Spolarich turned and looked intensely at Tyler, gesturing for him to stand up and reveal himself. But Tyler was frozen, humiliated. He'd fantasized repeatedly about how he'd bring Jungclaus to justice, how it would be this perfect moment like something out of a movie. But now that it was here, and not at all like Tyler had imagined, all he wanted to do was run away and hide. He suddenly noticed the crowd was laughing. It had started slowly, as the realization of just how insane the old man on the chair sounded, and began to sweep over the men, women and children in attendance. Within a few seconds, the entire room was thundering with laughter.

Jungclaus, who had now completely composed himself, looked right at Tyler and said with great sincerity, "My friend, I'm sorry I killed you... but you don't look any the worse for it!"

"Okay, Captain," Griffin yelled over the hoots from the crowd, "it's time to go."

The boys lifted the old man off the chair and escorted him quickly to the door, receiving some good natured pats on the back and few pieces of unsolicited advice about how they should monitor their grandfather's alcohol consumption. Captain Spolarich was furious.

"Why didn't you say anything?" he snapped at Tyler. "You could've told him!"

Griffin interjected. "Captain, what did you expect Tyler to say? You just made all three of us look like giant asses."

As they rapidly wound their way through the crowd in the parking lot, a booming voice called, "Stop there!"

Achim Jungclaus, who was being pursued by his wife, came lumbering up to them. The way his body quaked with anger and his large hands were curled into massive fists was clearly scaring the small, slender woman. Tyler felt something both sinister and familiar about his rage. The sensation was similar to how he had felt while watching the movie Old Acquaintance in Captain Spolarich's house.

"Achim, you really must stop!" Mrs. Jungclaus was half-pleading, half-demanding. "He's just a silly old man. Haven't we been embarrassed enough?"

Jungclaus turned to her a barked something in German. He then looked at Captain Spolarich like he was sizing up a cut of meat in a butcher's shop. "Who the hell are you?" he growled. "How dare you come into my club and behave like this!"

Captain Spolarich tapped his cane on the ground and set his jaw. Tyler had to hand it to the old man. He was fearless. Or ridiculous. Time would tell, he guessed. "I am Captain James Spolarich, U.S. Navy retired."

Tyler could see Jungclaus shuffling the name around in his head, trying to find a reference which was so very old. It didn't take long for him to realize who the Captain was and his expression suddenly fell.

"You think you can come here, after all this time, and disrespect me in front of my friends, my family?" he snarled.

"I wonder how much about your past your dear friends and family really know?" Captain Spolarich countered. "Not much, I would guess. Have you told them about the young man you killed at Fort Meade? How'd they react?"

"I didn't kill anyone. You tried to pin that on me once and it didn't stick. Now you pop up all these years later and try again." He looked at Tyler and his gaze made the boy shake. "And you drag these poor boys into it, as well?"

"There's no statute of limitation on murder," the Captain said.

"What stories has this old fool been telling you?" Jungclaus asked Tyler. "I remember you from a few weeks ago, you know. You came in and spoke to my wife. You told her you were doing research for school and you dropped a piece of paper with my name on it. Did your grandfather send you in there just to spy on me?"

"He's not my grandfather," Tyler said meekly.

"Thank your lucky stars for that, my boy," Jungclaus laughed cruelly. "The old man has some screws loose. What a story to tell!"

"Achim," Mrs. Jungclaus protested, touching his arm gently. "Let them leave. Or call the police and have them removed, but let's not give them one more moment of concern. We're having a party!"

Jungclaus shrugged her off. "No police," he said sternly. "But they came onto my property and behaved badly and I'll have my say about that."

"We're going to leave," Captain Spolarich said, "but I wanted you to know that you didn't get away with it. There are those of us who still remember what you did."

Jungclaus laughed. "Ah, yes, because your young friend here is really Tschantz, the traitor?"

There was a sudden and palatable electricity which rolled over all of them the moment the giant German spoke the name.

"So you do remember him?" Griffin said suddenly.

Jungclaus glared at him and snarled, "Get off my property!"

"But I am Ehren Tschantz," Tyler said, almost automatically. All four of them looked at him, speechless. Captain Spolarich smiled, but just a little. Tyler looked carefully at Jungclaus's face, searching for something there behind the brushy mustache and the deep wrinkles. "I remember you," he said.

The big man recoiled visibly. "What?" he grumbled.

Suddenly there was a flood of pictures rolling through Tyler's mind, like he was back at the Captain's house watching his DVD player on fast-forward and trying to make sense of all the disconnected images which were flying before his eyes. He saw a long room filled with whispering men and a felt as though he was desperately awaiting a rescue which never came. He remembered hushed voices in a dark room and a pressure he couldn't resist pressing down on him, crushing his face. He remembered fighting for air and finding nothing.

And then, to the astonishment of everyone, the thirteen-year-old said in flawless German: "You had the other men hold me down with blankets while you pushed a pillow over my face. You killed me as you had killed most of the men on board my boat when you cut those fuel lines."

"This's impossible," Jungclaus said, incredulous. A yellowish pallor suddenly spread across his face and he stumbled where he stood. "This's a trick!"

"It's no trick!" Tyler said, now in English. "And I'm no mouse!"

Jungclaus's anger had now changed to distress and Tyler felt it pouring off his body in a wave of intense heat. Suddenly, the boy realized just how important it was to leave. There was something in the big German's demeanor which had become inherently threatening, like an animal cornered by a hunter.

"We're leaving!" Tyler said, grabbing Griffin with one arm and Captain Spolarich with the other. "Don't come near us!"It took all his strength to half-pull, half-push the others to the car as both seemed to be in a daze. At his urging, Griffin started the engine and roared off, desperate to put as many miles as possible between them and an old memory which had become a sudden and frightening reality.

CHAPTER SIXTEEN

The week after Oktoberfest, Tyler called Captain Spolarich twice but their conversations were brief. Since his confrontation with Achim Jungclaus, the old man had been subdued to the point where Tyler thought he was heartsick. On the following Saturday, Tyler showed up for his usual community service work and was surprised to find the Captain actually had a list of chores for him to do. He'd come to expect that his service work would entail drinking bottles of cold root beer while flipping through the Captain's voluminous scrapbooks and talking about the war years. To his mind, the list of chores was further proof that there was something very wrong with the Captain.

After spending several hours sweeping and reorganizing the clutter on the old man's porch, Tyler wandered into the living room and found him in his recliner, draped with slumbering cats.

"Captain," Tyler said gently. "I'm done with the porch. What would you like me to do next?"

Spolarich looked up at him wearily. "Hmmm? What's that? You're done? Did you do a good job?"

"Yes, sir," Tyler answered.

"Well, why don't you call your brother and ask him to come pick you up. I think that's all I have for you today."

"Are you sure? I'm supposed to be here another two hours."

The Captain waved him off with a weak flick of his left hand.

Tyler stood there for a moment, ignored and nettled. "Aren't we going to do anything else about Ehren?" he asked. "About me?"

The Captain didn't look up when he answered. "What's more to do, Tyler?"

The boy shrugged. "I don't know. Something. I thought you didn't want Mr. Jungclaus to get away with this but now it seems like you don't care?"

The old man turned his head away and hid his eyes in his hand. "But he did get away with it, Tyler. We had our shot and they laughed at us. No one's gonna believe us now."

"That's true," Tyler said. He saw the Captain flinch a little as he said the words. "It's true because how we did it was unbelievable. Can you really blame all those people for laughing? We must've sounded ridiculous."

"You mean I must've sounded ridiculous."

"No, I mean all of us. Griffin and me, we were part of it too. We're a team. And as a team member, I am telling you that I don't want Jungclaus to get away with murder. He might be an old man but he's still a criminal who killed an innocent person."

The Captain's body shuddered slightly and it was obvious he was fighting back tears. "I'm sorry I got you involved in all this," he told Tyler. "It might've been better if I just had kept my big mouth shut."

"Maybe you remember that I came and found you?" Tyler said with an empathetic grin. "And you've helped me so much. I didn't know what was happening to me before I met you, and now everything seems so clear."

"But what I gave you was an awful truth," Spolarich groaned.

"But it was still the truth. Captain, do you know how screwed up I feel sometimes? I don't know who my father was and I haven't seen my mom in six years. I don't even know if she's dead or alive. My life's nothing but questions with no answers, but what few answers I have is thanks to knowing nice people who took care of me. Karen, Griffin, the librarian at my school, you..."

The Captain wiped his damp eyes with his thumb and answered weakly, "I don't know how else to help you. I don't know where to go from here. We'll never be allowed back on Jungclaus's property and now he'll be on guard. I guess I was hoping he'd just blurt out a confession when I confronted him. I was stupid. I'd forgotten how crafty he was. And, let's face it, I've lost my touch over the years. Used to be I could twist information out of any man anytime."

Tyler replied quietly, "Please don't give up on me. Everyone gives up on me."

The Captain smiled. "I haven't given up on you in over sixty years, but I'm lost as to how to help you now. Jungclaus will never confess, especially now that he knows we're watching him."

Tyler stood before the old man and felt miserable.

The Captain turned his face away again and said softly, "I just need time to think..."

The question of how to prove the unprovable bothered Tyler for the next few days as he struggled to fight off the sense of hopelessness that had already enveloped the Captain, and, to a lesser extent Griffin as well. By the end of the week, however, Tyler had decided that the spectacle they'd made of themselves at the Heidelberg Club was irrelevant. That they'd been laughed out of the place didn't change the fact that the murder of a young German man had taken place decades earlier was still considered unsolved. It didn't change the fact that the main suspect was still alive, at large and was now aware there were others who remembered his crime. It didn't change the fact that somehow, through some mechanism of fate or memory which none of them truly understood, Tyler had stood before Achim Jungclaus and had recited details of a past life in perfect German, a language he neither knew nor had had any previous contact with. Since the incident, Tyler had made numerous futile attempts to recreate his fluency in the language, sometimes just standing in front of the bathroom mirror and letting strange sounds roll off his tongue. But it all came out as complete gibberish.

With the enthusiasm of his teammates failing, Tyler decided to turn once again to the person who'd helped him without question. He walked in on Ms. Trease just as she was laying out her afternoon snack of fresh apple slices and Nutella. He swore he hadn't timed his entry into the library to specifically coincide with the introduction of food, but secretly wondered if his developing sixth sense had led him here without any conscious thought. Regardless, Ms. Trease was happy to share and even confided that the sliced apple was just a way of making herself feel less guilty about consuming great dollops of cocoa-hazelnut spread.

Tyler asked her, in his usual manner of offering no explanation for the question, if she thought it possible for someone to know a language without ever having learned it.

"Now that's an interesting thought," she said. "But I guess it goes back to the other research we've already done, doesn't it? It seems someone suddenly knowing a language they didn't know previously would be an example of an involuntary memory, where a person encounters some situation and suddenly memories they didn't know they had come bubbling back to the surface."

"But how would you know a whole language?" Tyler asked.

"That's the wonderful thing about this particular organ," Ms. Trease smiled, tapping Tyler's forehead with her fingertip. "Every bit of knowledge, every experience you ever have during your lifetime goes up there and is filed away. And it stays there forever. The problem we humans have is not in storing all that information, but in pulling those memories out when we need them. Recollection becomes harder as you age... which is why older people like me always have to write notes to ourselves."

"I have a friend who's very old," Tyler replied. "He's in his eighties and he remembers things which happened to him sixty years ago like they happened six minutes ago."

"That wouldn't be the man we called about the U-boats, would it? What's his name?"

"Captain Spolarich. Yes, that's him."

"How nice you became friends," Ms. Trease beamed. "Did he help you with your research?"

"Yeah. And now my brother and I go over and help him around his house. He's got a big place but can't do his yard work anymore."

"How nice of you!"

"So why do you think he remembers old events so clearly?"

"I think a lot of it has to do with what's important to you. Captain Spolarich probably recalls those really old memories so clearly because they're still important to him. Other newer memories which aren't important are pushed aside. But if you were someone who spoke Spanish all through your childhood, and then grew up and never spoke it again, you'd still know Spanish."

"So you would know it, even if you had forgotten how to speak it?"

"Exactly. Do you know who Mozart was?"

Tyler shook his head.

"Mozart was a great composer, an absolute musical genius. When he was only a toddler, he started playing the piano and took to it so quickly those around him thought he had some kind of supernatural ability."

"Did he?"

"Well, I'm not qualified to say, Tyler. My point is that if Mozart could understand something as complex as composing and playing music with virtually no training or experience, then I guess someone could take to a language very quickly as well."

Tyler paused, pensively drawing a large "E" on his plate in Nutella. "And do you think that if you were a reincarnated person, you'd still remember things like that from one lifetime to the next?"

"If you believe your memories and experiences would stay with you, attached to your soul as it moved from lifetime to lifetime, then yes, I think those memories could come bubbling up under the right circumstances. And that could include a forgotten language."

"But you couldn't ever prove something like that?"

Ms. Trease shrugged and took a deep breath. "I think you could prove the person in question didn't previously know the language, but it would be harder to prove that the sudden knowledge of the language was related to reincarnation. The belief in reincarnation is more a matter of faith, and faith is something that often defies proof."

Tyler was still reflecting on all this when the school's principal appeared at the doorway. Historically, the sudden appearance of a school administrator was bad news for Tyler. It usually signaled an impending detention or suspension. Sometimes it preceded a hostile interrogation about Tyler's knowledge of who had smashed ketchup packets all over the sidewalk or had thrown the girls' volleyball team's jerseys onto the school roof. This time, however, the principal seemed relieved to see Tyler.

"Tyler, have you been in here with Ms. Trease since school got out?" he asked. He was slightly out of breath and his brow was damp.

Tyler nodded.

"Oh, good, good," he said.

"Is something wrong?" Ms. Trease asked hesitantly.

The man came a sat on the edge of the table. "Tyler, do you have a grandfather who might come to the school looking for you?"

Tyler's mind immediately flashed to Captain Spolarich but he instinctively shook his head.

"Well, the yard monitors found a man in front of the school who said he was your grandfather and was here to pick you up. We couldn't remember you saying anything about a grandfather, so we thought it was a very strange thing for him to say."

"I don't have a grandfather," Tyler said.

"Could it be someone else?" Ms. Trease asked. "You just told me you have a friend who's in his eighties. Maybe it was him?"

Tyler shook his head. "He lives out of town and doesn't drive. What did this dude look like?"

"Well, he didn't look eighty," the principal said. "Or if he was, he's in great shape. He was a big man with a bald head and a big mustache. Do you know who that might be?"

Tyler sat frozen for what felt like an eternity and finally forced himself to shake his head.

"Are you sure?" Ms. Trease asked. She'd noticed his startled look.

"I'm sure. I don't know who that is."

The principal rose to his feet and said, "I'm going to ask you to stay here with Ms. Trease while I call your mom, okay? Please don't leave the school grounds until your mom comes to pick you up. We may need to have the police come down, too."

Tyler nodded. After the principal had left, Ms. Trease asked if Tyler wanted more apples with Nutella but he shook his head. He was no longer hungry. Suddenly, he just felt very afraid.

The police had taken a report from the school personnel about the mysterious old man who'd claimed to be Tyler's grandfather, but no one seemed to have any clue who he was or why he'd attempt something as risky as abducting a child from his school. Unfortunately, the school yard monitors had forgotten to obtain a license plate number on the man's car, although they described it as a silver luxury vehicle. Karen, who was understandably alarmed by the incident, had even called The Cowgirl to see if there was someone from Tyler's past who might be looking for him. The irony of that request was lost on everyone but Tyler and Griffin, but both boys were stuck with either revealing what they'd been up to with Captain Spolarich, or ignoring the fact that Achim Jungclaus clearly knew as much about Tyler as they knew about him.

"What I don't understand is how he found out who you are and where you go to school?" Griffin said as they swung together in his bedroom hammock.

"I was trying to remember if we said anything to him at Oktoberfest, like our names or whatever," Tyler frowned.

"Well, we might've used our real names but that wouldn't be enough for him to track you to your school. The Captain told him who he was and then you did that crazy little trick with speaking German. Did you tell him your name then?"

"To be honest, I really don't know what I said to him. It was like I was sleepwalking or something. I know I didn't give him the name of my school or anything."

"You know Mom wants me to take you and pick you up after school from now on. Maybe we should tell her who the old man is."

Tyler shook his head violently. "We can't, Griff. What if we get the Captain in trouble?"

"How'd we get him in trouble? He didn't do anything wrong."

"You know Karen will freak out when she finds out where we've been going and what we've been doing," he insisted. Griffin didn't look convinced so Tyler added, "I guess you can tell her if you really want to lose your car forever."

"Huh? She wouldn't take my car away. I'm nineteen. It's my car."

"You were breaking her rules and she's making the payments, Griff."

Griffin looked betrayed and cried, "Dude, that's not cool!"

Tyler shrugged. "Hey, I didn't say I was going to snitch you off. If she hears about it, or figures it out, it's because you can't keep your big mouth shut."

This stopped the debate. The two of them were quiet for a moment, then Griffin asked, "Tyler, if Jungclaus knows where you go to school, do you suppose he knows where you live too?"

The same impulse seized both of them and they scrambled up the spiraled iron stairs to the very top of the lighthouse, yanking open the defective padlock and stepping onto the circular platform where the light was housed. As long as you weren't scared of heights, the glassed-in room offered some of the best views in town. Looking east, north and south there was an uninterrupted view of the ocean and the entire coastline with its craggy cliffs and trees gnarled by the constant wind. Looking west you could see the entire expanse of Karen's property, the long driveway, the cistern, the crumbling maintenance shack, the nearby roads and even the northern end of town.

The boys stood at the thick glass and peered down.

"The school said he was driving a big, nice silver car," Tyler said.

"We should've brought binoculars," Griffin replied. After a moment he said, "Well, unless we camp out up here, there's no way of knowing if he'll come to the house. Besides, he probably won't risk it again. He lives too far away. He'd be missed."

"I think I'd take the risk if it meant keeping this kind of secret," Tyler said.

Griffin bit his lip. "Yeah. Good point."

Although there were no further incidents over the next week, both Tyler and Griffin continued to be on edge and would frequently climb the lighthouse stairs and survey the nearby roads for any suspect vehicles. Griffin and Karen would do the same whenever they dropped Tyler at school, sometimes going to the unusual lengths of driving through the parking lots and side streets in search of the elusive silver luxury car.

On Friday evening, Captain Spolarich called Tyler and asked him to come the following Sunday at precisely 1 p.m. to help him with some yard work. When he arrived, Tyler found the old man in better spirits than during his last visit. In fact, the Captain was busy watering the potted flowers scattered along his porch and front path.

"Captain, I can do that for you if you like?" Tyler said.

Spolarich shook his head and grinned. "It's good for the soul to get out in the sunshine and help living things grow, Tyler. The lawn could use a quick once-over with the mower, however."

Tyler nodded and walked obediently to the garage to fetch the mower. It was a heavily rusted contraption the Captain had owned since the 1950s. The blades were dull and it did an uneven job of cutting his grass, but the process seemed to make Spolarich feel like he was being productive. The garage, which hadn't contained a car in many years due to the Captain's failing eyesight, was full of cardboard boxes labeled in black marker and stacks of old furniture covered in tarpaulins. Tyler liked the garage. It was cool and dark and smelled like he imagined the oldest archives in the oldest museums must smell. But as Tyler was rolling out the lawnmower, he noticed the garage smelled differently. There was the faint but pungent aroma of smoke. Set off to one side was a galvanized bucket filled with the fragile black tissue of charred paper. Burnt matches littered the floor and several empty boxes were stacked nearby. The Captain had also piled dusty picture frames on the floor nearby, apparently having first removed and burned their contents. Tyler squatted down and poked through the ashes with a fingertip. Whatever the Captain had been burning, he'd done a thorough job. Tyler was only able to find a few recognizable fragments, which appeared to be scraps of old photographs or bits of newspaper.

As Tyler pushed the antique mower back to the front yard, the bucket full of ash continued to bother him. He parked the mower next to a tree and announced to the Captain that he needed to the use the bathroom before he started cutting the grass. He hurried inside the empty house and to the small upstairs room where Spolarich had shown him his collection of Ehren Tschantz artifacts weeks earlier. The room was virtually empty. The walls, once plastered with news articles and military memorabilia shoved into mismatched frames, were now bare with only the occasional nail or strand of steel wire to indicate anything had once hung there. The Captain's voluminous photo albums were all stacked together on a nearby table, but as Tyler flipped through them he found they too were either completely empty or much of their content had been removed.

Something began to well up inside Tyler. Something which he first mistook for anger, then realized was almost a sense of panic. The Captain had sanitized his entire house of any remnant or reminder of Ehren Tschantz or the murder which had haunted him for the last sixty years.

Tyler heard the front screen door bang shut and the slow, heavy shuffle of the Captain's feet. "Tyler!" the old man called. "Are you in here?"

The boy hesitated for a moment, unsure what to do with this new discovery. He considered hiding among the jumble until the Captain left, then sneaking out the house's back door. Perhaps he'd tell the Captain his delay in the bathroom was due to a bad batch of sausage he'd had for breakfast? Lies involving diarrhea were, in Tyler's experience, very effective. No body ever asked too many questions about diarrhea issues. But he was so tired of lies and deception.

He anchored his feet and yelled, "I'm up here, Captain!"

The old man tottered up the stairs and into the room, wiping his wet face with a wrinkled handkerchief. "I thought you were going to help with the mowing? You've been gone for ten minutes."

"I'm not the only thing that's gone missing, Captain," Tyler said defiantly, crossing his arms over his heaving chest. He could feel those old angry impulses bubbling to the surface. He felt like he needed to break something, but unfortunately the room was now cleared of anything breakable.

The Captain looked befuddled. "What's that you say?"

Tyler gestured widely at the empty walls. "What did you do? Everything's gone! All the evidence is gone!"

The Captain lowered himself into the room's only chair and sighed deeply. "Evidence of something we can't ever prove," he said.

"You don't know that," Tyler replied. "We messed up the first time. We came off sounding like a bunch of crazy people, but we can try again. We have to try again."

"I agree," the Captain said evenly.

Tyler was speechless for a moment. As was often the case when he interacted with the old man, he felt like the Captain was playing games with him. "You're confusing me," he exclaimed. "If you believe we should try again, then why'd you destroy everything?"

"Because when we try again we have to do it very differently."

"Huh?"

"The last time you were here, Tyler, I felt very down about what had happened at Oktoberfest..."

"Yes, I remember. But you also promised you wouldn't give up on this. You promised you wouldn't give up on me."

"And I'm keeping my promise."

"How?"

The Captain tapped his fingertips together pensively and said, "After we talked last week, I got to thinking that we don't need strangers to believe in your experiences. The only person we need to believe that you are Ehren Tschantz reincarnated is Achim Jungclaus."

"Well, I think he believes it, Captain. He came to my school this past Tuesday and told the yard monitors he was my grandpa and was there to pick me up. They chased him off and then the principal called the police. But they don't know who he was because no one got his license plate number and Griff and I have just been playing dumb. They know what his car looks like though."

The Captain chuckled, which wasn't the reaction Tyler was expecting.

"Captain," Tyler protested, "it's not funny, it's creepy. I don't want this old psycho stalking me!"

"It was necessary, Tyler."

"Necessary? What're you talking about?"

"If Jungclaus went to all the trouble to come to your school, it shows he believed what you told him at Oktoberfest. Or at least he's concerned enough to find you."

"So what do you think convinced him? Was it because I spoke to him in German?"

"I think it's what you said to him in German."

"But I don't even know what I said!"

"I know what you said," the Captain grinned. "You forget I speak German. That's why the Navy put me in the role of interrogating the P.O.W.s."

"So what'd I say?"

"You described how he killed you, putting a pillow over your face. And you told him you saw him cut the fuel lines to your U-boat. I don't know what that meant, but judging by the look on Jungclaus's face, you scared the heck out of him. And then, of course, you told him you weren't a mouse."

"What does that mean?" Tyler grumbled.

The Captain shrugged. "It doesn't matter what it meant. It seemed to do the trick because Jungclaus actually came to your school looking for you. It proved to him that you tapped into memories only two people in the world share — the murderer and his victim. That's what convinced him and that's what I'll use to catch him."

Tyler was still confused. Captain Spolarich seemed to be speaking in riddles and it was beginning to frustrate him. And then he came to a startling realization.

"Captain," he said, "did you tell Jungclaus who I was?"

The old man looked ashamed and didn't reply.

"You did!" Tyler cried. "That's what you meant when you said it was 'necessary' for him to find me at school."

"I figured school would be a safer place for that," the Captain responded. "You'd be surrounded by other kids and teachers and they'd protect you. But I needed to see if he believed enough to take the risk."

"Did you go back and see him after Oktoberfest?"

"No. He called me. He knew who I was so he looked me up in the phone book and called me up, just like you did. I told him I remembered his crime and I was going to see he paid for it. It was obvious from his tone we'd rattled his cage. He kept demanding to know who you were, so I told him to meet us at your school."

"What meeting? I didn't know about any meeting."

"That's because there wasn't one. I just told him that so he'd go to your school."

"Damn, Captain!" Tyler cried. "You set him up!"

Captain Spolarich nodded sheepishly. "I was hoping his visit to your school would be enough to have the police called on him, to have them start looking into who he was... But it sounds like he got spooked and took off."

"Geeze, Captain... I didn't know you were so devious."

"Remember, young man, my job during the war was counter-intelligence. It was my duty to always be thinking one step ahead of the enemy. Please believe me, Tyler, I didn't mean for any harm to come to you."

"Then why?" Tyler demanded.

"Because I know we'll never convict Jungclaus on a crime which happened so many years ago. The other conspirators are all dead and no court of law will ever believe you are the reincarnated spirit of Ehren Tschantz. In order to catch Achim Jungclaus, I only need him to believe he's about to be exposed. I need him to become so desperate to hide his old crime he's willing to commit a new crime. I am counting on him to be the same malicious animal today he was in 1945."

That sense of panic Tyler had felt earlier began to swell like a bubble in his chest. "Captain," he said grimly, "what're you planning?"

The old man rose to his feet and tapped his cane against the floor. "When the police arrive, don't tell them what used to be in here. Don't mention a word about reincarnation and tell your brother the same. No one will believe you."

"The police? Why are the police coming?"

The Captain hobbled to the door, turned and said, "All those years ago, I failed to protect you and then I failed to get you justice. But I promise I won't fail you again."

And with that, he slammed the door shut and quickly locked it. Tyler immediately leapt across the room and began yelling, "Captain! What're you doing! What's going on?"

"Stay quiet in there, Tyler," Spolarich called from the other side. "I'll tell the police where you are and they'll come and rescue you when it's over. Until then, stay quiet."

"Are you nuts? Let me out of here!" Tyler bellowed, beating his fists against the door. He could hear the Captain pushing furniture around and stacking piles of boxes, disguising the door among the other clutter of his home. Tyler continued to yell for help, but received no reply.

After several moments, he heard the front screen door bang shut and the house grew quiet.

CHAPTER SEVENTEEN

Captain Spolarich settled into his rocking chair on the front porch with his cane balanced across his knees and waited. Shortly before two o'clock, a long silver sedan pulled to a stop in front of the house and a hulking man with a bald head stepped out. The Captain had played out this confrontation a thousand times in his head and it had always concluded satisfactorily, but as the towering German strode up the path he suddenly felt an anger he hadn't experienced since 1945. There were two things he needed in order to be successful. The first was that Achim Jungclaus was disturbed enough by his experience with Tyler at Oktoberfest to be moved to panic. The second was that Tyler would stay quiet and secure in the hidden room. Of those two things, Spolarich had less faith in the second.

Jungclaus, who was only six years younger than Spolarich, had remained strong and robust as he had aged. He now towered before the Captain, still the brute he'd been at Fort Meade despite the years, the loss of his hair and the addition of a much larger belly. "Where's the boy?" he asked angrily.

The Captain smiled weakly and said, "He'll be here soon. Be patient."

"You told me to meet you at his school too, and then you never showed up. You'll regret it if you continue to play games with me."

"Patience. You've escaped prison for decades. Are you really so anxious to go now?"

The big German guffawed noisily. "You're a damn old fool, Spolarich. You weren't able to pin anything on me during the war, what makes you think you can do it now?"

"Because I have Tyler now."

"You have nothing. I don't know what you told him or how you coached him to put on that ridiculous performance at my club, but no one will ever believe you."

"You believe me," the Captain responded. "If you didn't, you wouldn't be here."

"I came to end this with you once and for all," Jungclaus growled.

"That's what I want too," the Captain replied. "You know, the police are already looking for you."

Jungclaus's arrogant expression suddenly fell. "That's a lie," he said. "Why would they be looking for me?"

"Because you showed up at Tyler's school and told the staff you were his grandfather. They didn't get your license plate number but plenty of people saw you and your pretty car. They're keen to talk to you from what I hear."

"You were the one who told me who he was."

"Well, that's your word against mine. You know, the police don't like it when strangers try to abduct children from school property."

"I didn't try to abduct anyone, you scoundrel," Jungclaus seethed. "You told me to meet you there!"

"Good luck proving that. And even if you could prove I set up that meeting, I certainly didn't tell you to pose as his grandfather. If nothing else, I bet the police will have a few questions about that. And once people start talking, who knows what'll start coming out. The next thing you know, the cops are looking into your background and they find out you were the main suspect in a murder case decades ago. That's not gonna look good to anyone. There's no statute of limitation on murder, you know. Whether you killed a man two minutes ago or sixty years ago, you can still go to prison for it."

Behind Jungclaus's dark eyes, Captain Spolarich could see the young man he'd interrogated so many years before. Arrogant. Fanatical. Heartless. The anger which had pitted these men against each other during the war was still there and it was beginning to boil.

"And your 'proof' of this murder is a boy who thinks he's the traitor Tschantz? No one will believe such an outrageous story," Jungclaus answered.

The Captain shrugged. "You managed to keep all your Nazi comrades quiet at the time, Jungclaus, but there was another witness to the murder and that was Ehren Tschantz himself. And Ehren's been very, very chatty."

"Liar!"

The Captain knew the level of danger was rising by the second, but he needed to push further. "Tell me something," he said calmly, almost condescendingly. "What did it mean when Tyler told you he wasn't a mouse?"

Jungclaus's eyes widened. The fact was, no matter how he tried to process that incident through his mind, there wasn't a person left alive who would've known what that meant. Just as there wasn't a person alive who could have witnessed him chop through the fuel lines which bound his U-boat to the refueling vessel in the middle of the Atlantic Ocean. The only witness to both of those events was a pile of bones buried and forgotten in the Fort Meade cemetery. As the years had progressed and the other P.O.W.s who had helped him murder Ehren Tschantz had died off, Jungclaus felt the danger recede. Now, suddenly, the entire experience was as fresh to him as though it had just happened.

The Captain pulled himself to his feet and took a step closer to the burly German. "What does it mean? What does 'mouse' mean? "

"Where's the boy?" Jungclaus growled.

This time, it was Spolarich's turn to smirk. Quietly, he turned and entered the house.

"Spolarich, where's the boy!" Jungclaus bellowed after him.

The Captain's legs didn't move as fast as he would've liked, but despite his infirmity and his poor eyesight, he knew the labyrinth of his house by heart and could maneuver it almost as well as his cats. The maze of antiques, clusters of furniture and piles of artwork and statuary would slow down even a young, healthy man. He was trusting it would slow down Jungclaus too.

As he expected, the big German had followed him inside and slammed the front door shut behind him. The noise sent the cats running for cover and had disturbed Tyler who was waiting impatiently to be released from the hidden room upstairs. Tyler ran to the door and pressed his ear against it. He could hear Jungclaus's booming voice and a wave of terror washed over him.

"Oh, no," he whispered to himself. "Captain, what're you doing?"

He turned and looked about the room. He had already done his best to escape through the door, but the Captain had secured it too well. As for the window, it was very small and looked out over a perilously sloping roof and a fifteen-foot drop to the yard below. Still, the window seemed like the only way out. Tyler began to struggle with a latch which had rusted shut years before when there was a thunderous crash on the first floor, as though the Captain's clutter was collapsing.

Spolarich had made it across the living room to the kitchen doorway, had turned, and using his rosewood cane like a crow-bar, had tipped over a large wood and glass bureau. The cane splintered and snapped as he pushed against it. The seven-foot tall cabinet toppled like a house of cards, sending shattered glass and porcelain flying across the room. The cabinet's upper edge came to rest on the arm of the couch, creating a barrier which Jungclaus would either have to climb over or crawl under. The Captain looked at the awe-struck German and smirked again. The fire inside Jungclaus was re-stoked.

The Captain hobbled over to the kitchen telephone, using the broken end of his cane to knock dishes, silverware and pans off the counter-tops and onto the floor, creating a tremendous racket in the process. Hopefully the neighbors would hear the noise and when the police entered the house, they'd find a mess which appeared to have been made by two men locked in hand-to-hand combat. He heard Jungclaus struggling to move the cabinet in the other room as he lifted the handset and dialed.

"9-1-1," a female voice answered. "What's your emergency?"

"Listen carefully," Spolarich said, "there's a man in my house named Achim Jungclaus. He's trying to kill me and a teenage boy named Tyler. We need the police to come quickly! The boy is hidden in a room upstairs. This man's insane!"

The operator's voice turned grim and urgent. "Okay, sir, we have your address. Is this man in your home now? Does he have any weapons?"

"He's in my home," the Captain cried as he heard Jungclaus clear the fallen cabinet with a flurry of crashes and profanity. "And he has my gun!"

And with that, the old man slammed the receiver back into its cradle and leaned against the kitchen counter as Jungclaus appeared in the doorway. With the fingers of his right hand he began to fumble for the nearby kitchen drawer.

"They're coming for you," Spolarich told the enraged man. "I'm going to tell them everything."

"They won't believe you," Jungclaus growled.

"Then maybe I'll have to finish this myself," he said, his fingers coiling around the drawer's handle and sliding it open to reveal the old U.S. military sidearm within. The weapon — a .45 automatic Colt pistol — was the same one he'd worn on his hip all through World War II, the same one he had worn during all those days and nights of interrogating Achim Jungclaus and getting nowhere. He'd kept it meticulously polished and cleaned through the years. It looked brand new.

He struggled to lift the heavy weapon. It was a desperately futile act coming from a man of his years, fragility and failing eyesight. He was no match for the younger, stronger Achim Jungclaus. It was the greatest bluff of his life. Years before, he'd tried every trick in his book to snap a confession out of the German submariner with no success. Today, he had to hope Jungclaus's rage and panic would do his work for him. He was not disappointed, as Jungclaus quickly grabbed the gun with his huge meaty hands and both men went tumbling onto the kitchen floor. The broken rosewood cane clattered across the tile as the two men struggled for control of the firearm, its muzzle tucked between their bodies and their clawing fingers. Captain Spolarich knew he couldn't match Jungclaus's physical power. In fact, he was counting on it.

There was a loud pop. It wasn't the kind of sound most people expected from a firearm's discharge. It sounded more like a champagne bottle being opened.

Jungclaus suddenly grappled to his feet and looked down on Spolarich, who was lying with his limbs twisted in a growing puddle of warm blood.

The Captain was able to conjure a feeble smile as he stared up at Jungclaus with tear-filled eyes. "I got you," he whispered.

Jungclaus stumbled back against the kitchen doorjamb. In the distance, he heard sirens. And then he heard something else. From above his head, somewhere on the second floor, he heard a boy beating against a door and shouting for Captain Spolarich.

After several minutes of crashing and shouting, the house had grown disturbingly quiet. Tyler could also hear the whine of the approaching sirens but as he pressed his face against the glass of the small window, still couldn't see any police cars. He tried prying open the window's latch again, but it was still sticking fast. There was then a creak behind the locked door, like a foot being placed on the stairs.

Tyler banged against the door again with a clenched fist. "Captain Spolarich!" he bellowed. "Are you all right? Answer me!"

Another creak. It was definitely coming from the stairway and for a instant Tyler thought his confinement to the small room was over. But the footfalls were too heavy for the Captain, and they were not accompanied by the usual rhythmic tap of his wooden cane. He rushed back to the window and tried the lock again. Still it wouldn't give.

A moment later the furniture and other clutter the Captain had piled in front of the door to disguise it began to shift, and Tyler felt his whole body seize up with fear. And there was something both familiar and terrible about his fear, like the other sensations he'd had when he stuck his head inside the old cistern near the lighthouse; then again at the Fort Meade graveyard; and most recently when confronted with Achim Jungclaus at the Oktoberfest celebration. He didn't take the time to recollect on or analyze this emotion. Instead, instinct guided him and he grabbed the room's only wooden chair and smashed its legs through the glass on the locked window. On the other side of the door, the barricade was being shifted faster. Boxes were being thrown aside and Tyler could hear the glass breaking on some of the framed prints the Captain had propped against the walls. He used the chair legs to crush as much of the glass as possible, then climbed clumsily onto the table top and squeezed his head and shoulders through the window frame. The shards of glass bit into his hands and arms and scraped through his hair and across the top of his scalp. A sticky wetness began to drizzle down the back of his neck.

Tyler had squirmed his upper body onto the slanted roof, struggling to find a hand-hold among the old wooden shingles now that his palms where filled with glass splinters. He pulled his legs through the opening, but it was like dragging them across a cheese-grater as the shards ripped into his denim jeans and through his knees and shins. He was now precariously positioned for a head-first tumble off the roof and into the Captain's vegetable garden. Then something seized his right foot around the ankle and with tremendous force began to drag him back through the window. Tyler pivoted to see Jungclaus's enraged face. One mammoth hand was anchored to Tyler's leg. The fingers were stained red.

The boy snapped his left foot against the side of the house and began to push back with all his might, ignoring for a moment the pain which was now cutting into his back. The old man was so strong. Just his size alone was enough to overwhelm a person, to immobilize them, to kill them. Jungclaus was trying to get his other arm through the narrow window frame, but his own girth was preventing it. Hoping to get a better grasp on Tyler, the man partially moved his head and shoulder out of the window. Tyler reacted quickly, removing his left foot from the side of the house and using it to deliver one hard, well-placed kick to the old man's face. There was a wet crunching noise and Tyler felt Jungclaus's nose break beneath the heel of his shoe. The powerful hand clenching his ankle was suddenly gone and the momentum sent Tyler tumbling backward across the rooftop. His fingers scratched uselessly at the shingles as he rolled toward the long drop ahead. And as the top of his head cleared the edge of the roof, and he felt himself become almost weightless for a moment, something tight and warm wrapped around his shoulders and chest. He flipped around as he hit the aluminum gutter at the roof's edge and was tossed away from the house to land hard in the barren, dusty garden below. The impact was cushioned, albeit slightly, by Griffin's rolling body as the young man made a somewhat ill-conceived attempt to catch Tyler before he hit the ground. Both of them lay in the sod, mouths filled of dirt and withered herbage, bleeding, gasping for breath, but very much alive.

Tyler sat up in a daze and looked up at the tiny window far above. Achim Jungclaus stared back at him, quietly, his eyes wide, astonished once again by a thirteen-year-old boy. His brushlike mustache was a bright scarlet from the blood cascading out of his nostrils, but he didn't seem to even notice the injury. He never blinked, never took his eyes off of the boys.

Tyler glanced over at Griffin as he awkwardly rolled onto his side. Griffin's mouth was full of blood and his two front teeth were loose.

"Where'd you come from?" Tyler asked.

"It's after two o'clock," Griffin choked. "It's time to go home."

"You keep rescuing me," Tyler smiled weakly.

"You keep making me," Griffin responded.

There was a loud pop and Tyler felt a puff of hot air hit his face as a bullet zipped over his left shoulder and buried itself in the garden sod nearby.

"Run!" he shouted to Griffin, grabbing the older boy by the elbow and heaving him to his feet. Jungclaus clumsily lined up another shot through the narrow window and squeezed the trigger. The Colt .45 kicked and the bullet smashed through two wooden roof shingles before hitting the ground several feet from the running boys. Tyler and Griffin ducked to their right, concealing themselves under the house's eaves.

"That's him, right?" Griffin gasped. "That's Jungclaus?"

Tyler nodded.

"What the hell is he doing here?"

"It was a trap. The Captain wants Jungclaus to murder him!"

"What? Why?"

"He doesn't think we'll ever be able to prove the murder from Fort Meade. So the Captain's decided to create a new one. His own!"

"We need to get out of here. Run for my car."

Tyler grabbed his brother's arm before he could move. "Griff," he said, "the Captain's still inside. We can't leave him."

"The cops will help him."

"What if that's too late?" Tyler cried, but he wasn't waiting for Griffin to reply or protest. He was already scrambling toward the back door of the house.

Both of the boys nearly tripped over the Captain as they entered the kitchen, and Tyler slipped in the puddle of blood which had collected on the floor between the refrigerator and the stove, knocking a stack of dishes onto the floor. The old man had pulled himself into an awkward sitting position. A wound in his shoulder, about the diameter of a penny, was producing a steady rivulet of blood that had soaked his shirt and created an ugly scarlet smear across the front of the kitchen cabinets.

The old man was still alive and even managed to conjure a smile at the sight of them.

"Get out of here!" he whispered, his breathing heavy and wheezing.

"We're taking you with us," Tyler replied. "Can you walk?"

Overhead, Jungclaus's heavy footsteps began to reverberate as he ran toward the stairs. Captain Spolarich grabbed Tyler's hand and squeezed it hard.

"You have to run!" he grimaced.

Tyler glanced at Griffin and then commanded, "Griff, you get the Captain out. I'll slow down Jungclaus."

"No you won't! Get out of the house right now!" Griffin barked, but it was too late as Tyler was already clambering over the broken bureau which had partially blocked the kitchen doorway from the living room side.

He paused for a moment in the splintered ruins of home. Through the lacy curtains which covered the front windows, he saw the flashing lights of several police cars pull to a stop and officers in dark uniforms begin to quickly fan across the yard. The heavy footsteps from the second floor had stopped, and other than the irritated grunts from Griffin as he half-carried, half-dragged Captain Spolarich toward the kitchen door, the old house was again strangely silent. Even the Captain's numerous cats were nowhere to be seen, having sought cover with the first crash.

Tyler took two steps forward, trying to make as little noise as possible but the floor was covered with shards of glass which crunched beneath his weight. He reached the bottom of the stairs, knelt down and peered around the wooden banister. A dark shape moved at the top of the stairs, there was a flash of light and another bullet zipped passed him. Tyler recoiled immediately, banging against the broken bureau.

Outside the house, the assembling police officers ducked for cover. "Shots fired! Shot fired!" someone yelled.

"I know where you are!" Jungclaus called from above, keeping the barrel of the gun fixed on the landing below.

"Do you know who I am?" Tyler called back. His voice broke and skipped.

Jungclaus paused. "How'd you do it?" he asked.

"I don't know," Tyler replied. "I guess it doesn't matter. You're going to jail."

"Not yet," the old German chuckled. "If I kill you again today, maybe we'll meet up in another sixty years? Maybe we'll just keep playing this out for a thousand more lifetimes?"

"I don't think so," Tyler growled. "Twice was enough for me."

Tyler pulled himself back into a crouch. Above his head, he heard Jungclaus shift as well, waiting for his next move. He couldn't stay where he was, trapped between the banister and the fallen wooden bureau. The moment Jungclaus came down the stairs, he'd have no cover. He noticed the lower half of Captain Spolarich's broken cane lying on the floor nearby. The broken end formed a sharp point. He snatched it up and leapt across the bottom of the stairwell. Two more bullets ripped into the floorboards, sending up tiny showers of wood splinters. The shots were quickly followed by Jungclaus rushing down the stairs, his massive frame shaking the floor under Tyler's feet. Tyler leapt over the back of a Victorian armchair and tumbled onto the floor. Then, scuttling about on his hands and knees, he crawled behind piles of stacked artwork and other collectibles, dislodging several of the Captain's cats from their hiding spots. The animals sprinted off for new cover, momentarily distracting Jungclaus. Tyler pulled himself into a ball and tucked himself between the legs of a small end table and a large oil painting of rain clouds over a desert choked with cactus. All those years of hiding behind the boxwood shrubs took on a practical value and suddenly Tyler didn't feel like an awkward and impetuous boy teachers groaned about and other kids avoided. Suddenly, he felt like he had more purpose than anyone else in the world. To his surprise, that purpose really wasn't about bringing Achim Jungclaus to justice. It was about delaying the killer long enough for Griffin and Captain Sporlarich to reach safety.

He held his breath and listened to for the big German. Again the house was quiet. There were no more grunts and bangs from the kitchen, which meant Griffin and the Captain had escaped.

Outside, a voice blared over a loudspeaker. "You in the house! This's the police! Leave any weapons inside and come out the front door with your hands raised!"

Jungclaus paused among the rubble of the living room, adjusting his grip on the hot, wet handle of the . 45. The police request was laughable. After all these years, could anyone really expect him to just surrender himself?

"I know where you are," he whispered to the silent room.

It was a bluff and Tyler knew it. The oil painting would not protect him from a bullet, but for the moment, his silence would.

Jungclaus took several more steps toward the far side of the room. The muzzle of the gun skipped from place to place, looking for a target. A thirteen-year-old wouldn't have too many places to hide, he told himself.

He took two more steps and suddenly a pain like he had never felt before brought him to his knees. There was a sickening sound, like heavy cloth being ripped in two and a hot font of fresh blood sprayed across the floor. Jungclaus glanced down at the broken rosewood cane which had been thrust through the calf of his left leg. A large hunk of muscle and bloody tissue hung off the spear-like tip. In his agony, he dropped the pistol and a small, quick hand darted out from behind an oil painting and snatched it off the floor. Jungclaus grabbed the painting's frame and flung it away, but the boy, who seemed unnaturally adept at squeezing and crawling between the mounds of bric-a-brac, was already scrambling away.

Tyler hopped behind a bookcase arranged with Egyptian figurines and cradled the gun in his hands. It was so hot it was nearly unbearable to touch. He peeked around the edge of the bookcase and saw Jungclaus floundering like a bird with a broken wing. The man was groaning and cursing in slurred German. He couldn't walk, and was struggling to even stay upright.

"I'm going to find you!" Jungclaus yelled out. "I will kill you again! I will kill you a hundred more times if that's what it takes!"

It may take a hundred more times, Tyler thought. He shifted the Colt .45, positioning it firmly in the fingers of his right hand. For the first time in all his encounters with Achim Jungclaus, the big German was helpless. Tyler took just a second to wonder how others might handle such an opportunity, if they suddenly had complete control over a murderer's fate. He knew what Jungclaus would do if the tables were turned. The old man had already demonstrated his merciless nature with the numbers of deaths he'd caused over the years: Ehren Tschantz's crewmates who were left to burn or drown when Jungclaus cut the fuel lines to their U-boat; Tschantz himself, smothered in his bed; and perhaps Captain Spolarich as well. But Tyler was not Jungclaus, and if there was any fragment of Ehren Tschantz inside of him, it too was guiding his choices.

The boy stood up and aimed the gun at Jungclaus. The old man glared at him, defiant even at the moment of defeat.

"Kill me if you can," Jungclaus growled.

"I can," Tyler replied calmly, "but that's not what I do. Not in 1945, and not now."

Without saying another word, the teenager quickly skirted the edge of the room, keeping the gunsight trained on the old German. He scrambled over the toppled bureau and dropped the gun into the kitchen trash can. Then he flung open the back door of the house and ran to join his brother and Captain Spolarich behind the line of police cars.

CHAPTER EIGHTEEN

Tyler was sitting behind a row of boxwood shrubs waiting for the new kid to arrive. It was the first new child to be placed at Karen's lighthouse since Sawyer had departed three months earlier. Everyone had decided, and Tyler had agreed, that after the recent events it was better to just let him enjoy the undivided attention of his mother and brother before bringing in another foster child. The three of them had visited Captain Spolarich in the hospital almost daily; and spent the weekends cleaning up his messy house and caring for his menagerie of cats. When the old man was finally able to return home, he found the place immaculate. Griffin even patched all the bullet holes so they were unnoticeable.

The Cowgirl and a police detective had been out to interview Tyler after the arrest of Achim Jungclaus. "I know you went with Captain Spolarich to a German-American fair, correct?" the detective asked Tyler.

"Oktoberfest," Tyler said.

"Yes. That's right. I know Jungclaus and Spolarich had some kind of altercation there."

"Does that mean they had a fight?"

"Well, an argument. Do you remember that?"

"Yes, I remember. Captain Spolarich recognized Mr. Jungclaus as a man he thought had killed someone many years ago."

"In a camp for German prisoners of war?"

"Yes. During World War II. The Captain had investigated the crime but was never able to prove that Mr. Jungclaus had done it. The Captain called him out on it and Mr. Jungclaus got really mad about it. He kicked us out of the fair."

The detective scribbled a few notes on a pad of paper and furrowed his brow. "Tyler, do you have any idea why Mr. Jungclaus might think you were a German sailor he knew over sixty years ago?"

Tyler shrugged. "Maybe he was crazy?" he suggested. "'Cause I'm only thirteen... almost fourteen."

The detective chuckled. "Well, I guess someone else can figure that out. It would've been kind of hard for you to have been around for that long, wouldn't it? Unless you're a lot older than you look?"

Tyler nodded. "What's going to happen to Mr. Jungclaus?" he asked.

The detective sighed and said, "Well, he's in a lot of trouble. He shot one person and tried to kill you and your brother as well. He's an old man who's probably going to die in prison."

Tyler nodded grimly.

"How're you doing with all this, Tyler?" the Cowgirl asked. "This had to be a very frightening experience for you."

Tyler thought about his answer for a moment. "I'm fine," he said assertively. "My family's been there for me all the way. So, yes, I'm fine."

The Cowgirl smiled. For the first time since she'd known him and asked him how he was, she actually believed his answer.

Tyler never saw the detective again; and no one ever asked him again about prison camps, U-boats or a man named Ehren Tschantz. The would-be murderer was still making his absurd claims that Tyler was the reincarnated spirit of a dead German submariner, but no one was listening.

Now Tyler sat hunkered down behind the boxwood shrubs. He was almost too large to fit in the space between the house and the plants anymore. He'd need to find a new spot to observe the world.

Maybe I'll start going more to the top of the lighthouse, he mused. The view's much better up there anyway.

The front door slammed and footfalls quickly crossed the porch and bounded down the steps. Griffin rattled the branches on the shrub.

"Are you back there?" he asked.

"Yeah," Tyler said.

"The new kid's going to be here any minute. You're not going to hide for this, are you?"

Tyler thought about it for a moment, but it was only for dramatic effect. "No," he replied. "I'm coming out."

AUTHOR'S NOTE

This story is fictional, but was based on actual events and circumstances which occurred during the last years of World War II. It was not uncommon for Allied forces, particularly the British and Americans, to work with captured German prisoners to extract information about troop movements, enemy technology and battlefield strategy. During the last year of the European war, more and more captured Germans were willing to help the Allies or expressed anti-Nazi sentiment. From January 1944 through the end of July 1945, American forces estimated that as much as 44% of the German P.O.W.s in custody were anti-Nazi. This may have been due to a harsh realization about Adolf Hitler and his government. As the war steadily turned against the Germans, the Nazi leadership set out to punish its own people for their battlefield losses. Hitler himself ordered a "scorched earth policy" be carried out on German soil, burning entire towns, fields and other infrastructure to the ground so it couldn't be used by the advancing Allies or even the German people. Hitler was never able to admit his own insane leadership brought about the destruction of Germany. Instead, he blamed the German people. The man who rallied so many Germans with promises of military conquest and the myth of being a superior race did, in the end, betray them utterly.

Even before the imminent defeat of the Nazis, however, many ordinary Germans suffered terribly at the hands of their own government. How a person chose to believe, speak, worship or vote could mean imprisonment or death. Many of the young men forced to enlist in Hitler's army and navy probably had friends or family members who had vanished, had been falsely imprisoned, or had been murdered. These men were particular valuable to the Allies and many, like the fictional character of Ehren Tschantz, became willing traitors to their own nation in service of a greater good. Like Tschantz, they saw the destruction of the evil Nazi empire as being necessary if Germany — and freedom — was going to survive in Europe and throughout the world. Although they are rarely given credit for the sacrifices they made, these men (called "stool pigeons" by the Americans) helped bring about the successful conclusion of the war and the destruction of the Nazi empire.

Marsh Myers

ABOUT THE AUTHOR

Marsh Myers is a writer, artist, filmmaker and self-described arrested adolescent. The adoptive father of two boys and former foster parent of many others, the character of Tyler in HIS LIFE ABIDING was lifted from Marsh's years of experience dealing with special needs children. The book's paranormal themes also reflect Marsh's interest in the mysterious and unknown. These themes can be found in his other works, including his online collection of short stories called Tiny Tales of the Mostly Macabre.

You're invited to visit **marshmyers.com** and enjoy additional features related to creative writing, art, film and photography.

UPCOMING RELEASE

Watch for this new young adult novel from Marsh Myers arriving soon.

THE MEN IN THE TREES

Meryl Panagos has no time for monsters. While other girls her age are enjoying high school dances and their first crushes, Meryl's living on her own and struggling to raise her young son in a small Oregon town. Although she has a good job at a friend's comic book store, it's difficult to make ends meet while saving enough money to begin classes at Oregon State University.

But when her ad for a roommate is answered by Rose Washington, it seems like the perfect solution to Meryl's money issues. Rose is a retired school teacher with plenty of cash on hand and a willingness to cook, clean and even babysit when needed. She seems like the perfect surrogate grandmother — until Meryl discovers the real reason she moved to Oregon—

Rose is searching for a long lost gold mine hidden in the sprawling forest nearby!

As bizarre as it seems for a sixty-year-old woman to be treasure hunting, the tale behind the gold mine is even stranger. Did some band unknown forest creatures attack the mine over a century ago — forcing the soul survivor to flee Oregon and never return? Spurred on as much by this ancient mystery as the promise of great wealth, Meryl finds herself entangled in Rose's quest.

But the vast forests of the Pacific Northwest hold many secrets... and some don't wish to be discovered!

Made in the USA
Lexington, KY
27 May 2013